LARGE PRINT LEN
Lennox, Marion.
A royal proposition

A ROYAL
PROPOSITION

A ROYAL PROPOSITION

BY

MARION LENNOX

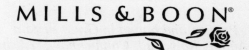

To David,
who took my heart to Paris.

All the characters in this book have no existence outside the imagination of the author, and have no relation whatsoever to anyone bearing the same name or names. They are not even distantly inspired by any individual known or unknown to the author, and all the incidents are pure invention.

*First published in Great Britain 2002
Large Print edition 2003
Harlequin Mills & Boon Limited,
Eton House, 18-24 Paradise Road,
Richmond, Surrey TW9 1SR*

© *Marion Lennox* 2002

ISBN 0 263 17874 9

*Set in Times Roman 16¼ on 17 pt.
16-0103-54741*

*Printed and bound in Great Britain
by Antony Rowe Ltd, Chippenham, Wiltshire*

CHAPTER ONE

'ALASTAIR, I know you and Belle are planning to marry, but you *must* marry Penny-Rose first.'

Silence. Marguerite de Castaliae looked as unruffled as if she'd just talked of the weather, but Alastair and Belle were staring at her as if she'd dropped a bomb.

'What are you saying?' It was Alastair who first found his voice. His Serene Highness, Alastair, Prince de Castaliae dug his hands deep into the pockets of his faded jeans. His dark eyes closed. What now? He didn't need his mother making crazy propositions. Not when he had so much else to think of...

If this inheritance didn't go through, the village faced ruin. After months of effort, he'd found no way to save it. His own fortune couldn't save this place. Nothing could.

Today he'd reached a final, joyless decision. He'd been up since dawn inspecting the cattle with stock agents, working out how much they'd make at market. He'd come in to make a final bleak phone call to his accountants.

They'd given him their verdict and it was all looking futile.

The banks would never finance such a venture. The estate would have to be sold.

So Alastair was exhausted, and he didn't need this.

'Marry someone else? That's ridiculous.'

'It's not ridiculous.' His mother was wearing her I'm-about-to-solve-all-your-problems smile. 'My dear, you do *want* to be a prince?' She was probing, fishing for a reaction.

She found it. 'No!' Alastair turned to stare out the window, over the castle's lush gardens to the river beyond. 'No,' he said again. His voice was surer still, and there was revulsion in his tone. 'It was Louis who was supposed to inherit all this. Not me.'

'But Louis is dead, dear,' Marguerite reminded him. 'And I won't even pretend I'm sorry, because he would have made a very bad prince. If he'd inherited...'

'It was his right to inherit.'

'He drank that right away,' his mother retorted. 'He was a wastrel and a fool, and now he's dead. So now the title is yours. And the responsibilities.'

'I never wanted it.'

'But it's yours for the taking.' Marguerite's gaze shifted from her son to her future daughter-in-law, and her probing eyes were thoughtful. 'If you want it badly enough,' she said gently. 'And if Belle wants it.' Her voice became questioning again. 'I'd imagine Belle would rather like to own this castle and be your princess?'

'Belle doesn't care about titles,' Alastair said shortly. 'Just as I don't.'

Marguerite wasn't as sure of that as her son was, but she kept her face deliberately expressionless. This tiny Castaliae principality, tucked between France and the rest of Europe, might be a very small player on the world stage, but it was a lovely place to live—and maybe a wonderful place to rule?

Wealth and position might very well appeal to Belle, she thought, but she'd have to use other ways to persuade her son.

'Alastair, the people here need you,' she told him. 'The country is depending on you.'

'We've been over this.'

'Yes, dear, but you're not listening. If you don't inherit, there's no one else to take it on.' These were hard facts to be faced, and the sooner her son faced them the better.

'If you don't accept it, the estate will be carved up and the title will disappear,' she told him. 'Most of the people who've lived here all their lives will face losing their own homes. Then the village houses will be bought by holidaymakers who'll only live here for three or four weekends a year.'

'No!' said Alastair, outraged.

'Of course not. None of us want that.' She was getting through. All she could see of her son was his strongly muscled back, but it was expressive enough. Alastair had been brought up to accept responsibility. Marguerite had every hope that he'd accept it now.

Despite Belle.

Or even with Belle's assistance...

Alastair was a good son, she thought fondly. A son to be proud of. Until his recent involvement with Belle, Alastair de Castaliae had been considered to be one of Europe's most eligible bachelors.

Well, why not? Of royal blood and with an inherited fortune, he'd been attractive even as a child. Time had added to his good looks until, at thirty-two, his mother—and a fair percentage of the principality's female population—considered him perfectly splendid.

The tragedy in his background did nothing to lessen his appeal. In fact, the distance he'd placed between himself and the rest of the world since Lissa's death had seemed only to make him more desirable.

And he *was* desirable, his mother decided, trying to look at him without bias. Alastair was six feet two in his socks—and his muscled, taut and tanned frame made him seem even taller. He was smoulderingly dark. His jet black hair, his crinkling, brown eyes and his wide, white smile had made many a girl's heart melt.

Just as his father's smile had melted her own heart all those years ago...

Sternly Marguerite blinked back unexpected tears and returned to the job at hand. Emotion wasn't any use here. It wouldn't convince Alastair—he'd held himself emotionally distant after Lissa died—and she was almost convinced that Belle didn't have any emotion to play with.

'It's only for a year.'

'What's only for a year?' Alastair turned back to face his mother, his brow drawn heavily over his deep-set eyes. 'You sound as if you have this whole thing arranged.'

'Well, I do,' she said apologetically. 'Some- one has to think of the future. You've been so involved getting the estate back into working order—making sure all the workers are paid, organising the rebuilding of the stonework, doing all the work caused by two such sudden deaths—that you haven't had time to look at the whole picture. So if you'll only listen...'

'I'm listening.'

It was the best she could hope for, but he was still glowering. And all she could do was explain.

'Our problems are all caused by Louis's father changing the inheritance,' she told him. 'Louis's dissolute ways were giving him nightmares, so he put in the clause—'

'I know this.' Of course he knew. After all, Louis had bleated to him of it often enough, and the clause was the nub of his problems now. Alastair's brow descended even further. 'It decreed that Louis marry a woman of unimpeachable virtue or he couldn't inherit.'

'Yes.' Marguerite tried very hard not to look at Belle. What she was about to say now wouldn't be easy. Alastair already understood about the clause—but did Belle? 'Your uncle couldn't predict that Louis would end up in the grave three months after his own death. And now it's left us in a mess, because the clause applies to anyone inheriting the title—which includes you.'

Silence. Then...

'Contrary to what the lawyers are saying,' Alastair said softly, in a voice that sounded almost dangerous, 'Belle *is* a woman of unimpeachable virtue.'

'No, dear, she's not.' Marguerite refused to be silenced. There was no easy way to say this but both Belle and Alastair had to face it. She'd been saving it for when Alastair saw how bleak his position was, and that time was now.

'You know it, or you wouldn't be spending all this time with the accountants,' she went on. 'The lawyers are all of the same opinion. Your cousins are prepared to take legal action to see that the estate's sold and divided, and if you marry Belle that's exactly what will happen.'

'Just because Belle's been married before—'

'And also because she's had affairs, ever since she was a teenager.' Marguerite did look at Belle now, and her tone softened. 'I'm sorry, my dear,' she told her, 'but it's time for plain speaking.'

'Go right ahead,' Belle told her. Alastair's companion sat with her hands loosely clasped on her elegantly crossed knees. She was wearing a chic, black dress, her silk-stockinged legs looked as if they went on for ever and her expression, rather than seeming offended, seemed coolly calculating. She tilted her head, causing her sleek bob of auburn hair to glint in the sunlight. It made a striking impression, and she knew it. 'So I'm not a woman of unimpeachable virtue. Fine. Don't mind me.'

'I do mind you, dear,' Marguerite said apologetically. 'But the cousins have been digging up dirt. I gather you had an affair with a married man when his wife was pregnant...'

Belle's beautiful face shuttered down at that. 'That was ten years ago. It's hardly relevant.'

'The lawyers say it is. And it means that if Alastair marries you, he can't inherit.'

'Which is damnable,' Alastair snapped, and his mother nodded in agreement. But her face didn't look hopeless.

'Yes, dear, it is damnable, but it's also avoidable.'

'I'm marrying Belle!'

'But if you waited for a little—'

'No.'

'Just a moment.' Belle rose, stretched, cat-like, and crossed to where Alastair was standing. And as she did, his mother had to acknowledge why her son had been attracted to her.

Falling in love had never been an issue for Alastair. Not after Lissa. However, he'd rarely been without a beautiful companion, and Belle was certainly beautiful. She was magnificently groomed and chic and incredibly feminine. She spoke three languages, which, in this tiny border principality, was a huge advantage, and her social skills were polished to perfection. Even in Alastair's present occupation as a Paris architect, she'd be a hostess to be proud of.

Belle was sleek and feline and clever, and she'd spent a lot of effort persuading Alastair that marriage could suit them both. For maybe the hundredth time, Marguerite wondered how she could get on with such a daughter-in-law.

But Belle wasn't thinking of marriage now— at least, not her own. Not yet. She laid one beautifully manicured finger on Alastair's arm and turned to face Marguerite, her intelligence focussed. 'Tell us your plan,' she said softly, and with a stab of triumph Marguerite realised just how hungry for the title this woman was.

She'd thought that she would be. Married to Alastair while he worked as a Paris architect, Belle would have had wealth and position, but here was the chance of more. With the death of Louis—with the chance of inheriting this magnificent estate—came the title of Prince and Princess and money to keep them in unimaginable luxury for the rest of their lives. It was a windfall Belle would reach out and grasp with both hands.

If she could.

But the old man's will stood between them. *'A woman of unimpeachable virtue...'*

'Tell us your plan,' Belle said again, and it was as much as Marguerite could do not to sigh with relief. She sat back and closed her eyes for one millisecond—to give her enough space to gather her thoughts. Then she started.

'Penny-Rose,' she said.

'Who's Penny-Rose?' Alastair demanded.

'The woman you need to marry. For a year.'

Penny-Rose O'Shea settled the final stone into the dirt with a satisfied slap. Great. Finished! It had taken her all morning to choose the slabs that would be the foundation of her wall. It was immensely satisfying work, and Penny-Rose was satisfied.

She was also extremely hot.

Midday had arrived without her realising. She put up a hand to wipe sweat from her face, and felt ingrained dirt smudge thickly across her cheek. Urk! A beauty queen she wasn't!

Never mind. It was good, honest dirt, she thought happily. She was doing what she wanted to do, and by evening she'd be even dirtier. Also, she'd have the next layer of stones complete. Building walls designed to last a thousand years might not be everyone's cup of tea, but it was hers and she loved it.

'Penny-Rose!' She looked up to find her boss waving to her from the other end of the wall.

Was he reminding her of lunch? That was strange. Bert didn't usually remind his workers it was time to knock off, but she rose gratefully to her feet.

But he wasn't reminding her of lunch.

'You're wanted,' he told her, thumbing toward the castle. 'By them indoors.'

'What?'

'You heard what I said.' Bert's weather-worn face creased even further with a puzzlement that matched hers. 'Someone came out just now and said could we send you inside. Pronto. There's no mistake.'

'They want me to go inside?' Penny-Rose stared at her boss in disbelief, and then stared down at herself. She was wearing begrimed overalls, her shoulder-length chestnut curls were twisted into a knot under her filthy cap and every inch of her was covered with dust. She grimaced. 'Why?'

'They sent a message saying they want to see you, and that's all I know,' her boss said patiently.

'You're kidding.' She glanced up at the forbidding ancestral home, where those who'd issued the summons were hidden.

'They can see me by looking out their windows,' she told her boss, and she grinned. 'That way I won't besmirch their ancestral floors.'

'Don't be clever, lass.' Bert, normally the kindest of bosses, was perturbed and it showed. 'I don't know what they want, and I can't say I like it. Do you want me to come in with you?'

'Yeah, take him with you, Penny-Rose,' one of the lads called. The whole stone-walling team was fascinated at this unexpected twist of events, and the cheekiest of the men came to his own conclusion. 'Maybe the new prince has decided to increase his harem.'

'Or maybe that other one—what's her name, Belle? Maybe she thinks our Penny-Rose is prettier and she's decided to tear her eyes out,' another added, and his comment was greeted by hoots of laughter.

The entire team was in on the conversation now. They were all male, mostly a lot older than Penny-Rose, and concern for their protégée was behind their good-natured banter.

'How would they know our Penny-Rose is prettier? *We* only see her for five minutes every morning before the dust settles back,' one demanded.

'She is pretty, though,' the first lad said stubbornly. 'Real pretty. If the prince saw her without her dirt…'

'Well, he hasn't.'

'His mother has.'

'Not without her dirt, and, anyway, what's that got to do with the price of eggs?'

'No, lass…' Bert cut across the banter and his eyes were still troubled. 'Seriously, they've asked to see you. You spoke to the old lady, didn't you? You didn't say anything to upset her?'

'No.' Penny-Rose wiped filthy hands on her overalls, thinking fast. 'At least, I don't think so.'

Penny-Rose had arrived at the castle with the team of Yorkshire stone-wallers six weeks ago, and she'd had her hands full ever since. There was so much to be done! After years of neglect, the west farmyard walls had almost entirely collapsed, and if they weren't mended soon, the north and south walls would do the same.

So she hadn't had time for socialising. The only contact she'd had with the titled landholders had been a conversation with the castle's elderly mistress.

Marguerite had been out walking, and had come across a stooped figure sorting stones. 'Good heavens, it's a girl,' the woman had said, startled, and Penny-Rose had chuckled. She'd deferentially hauled off her cap, letting her curls tumble to her shoulders.

'Yes, ma'am.'

'You're part of the stone-walling team?' the woman had demanded, her amazement deepening, and Rose had smiled and once more agreed.

'That's right.'

'But the team's from Yorkshire.'

'And I'm not from Yorkshire.'

'Now, how did I guess that? Where are you from?'

'Australia.'

'Australia!' The woman's eyes had still been creased in astonishment. 'Why on earth are you here?'

'I'm working with the best stone-wallers in the world,' Penny-Rose had told her, not without pride. 'I'm gaining my master-waller's certificate, and when I'm finished training, I can go home and demand my price.'

Then Penny-Rose had looked up at the castle where the soft gold sandstone turrets and battlements shone in all their glory, as they'd shone for almost a thousand years. Her green eyes had twinkled in appreciation of the beauty around her.

'It's great work,' she'd said softly. 'It almost makes up for having to work in the shadow of rickety old shanties like this.'

The woman laughed, seeming genuinely amused. She stayed for some time, seemingly intrigued by Penny-Rose's work. Her questions were gently probing, but maybe it was her right to probe the background of workers on her son's estate. Penny-Rose thought no more of it, and when the woman left, she felt as if she'd made a new friend.

But now...

Had she taken her joking seriously? Was she about to send a message through Penny-Rose that the team was no longer required?

Help...

'Do you want me to come in with you?' Bert asked again, her worry mirrored in his eyes. This was an important job, and both of them knew there was a lot at stake. 'Not that I think you have any need to worry, but I can't think of any reason they'd want you.'

'They're hardly likely to toss me into the ou-bliette for insubordination.'

'Have you been insubordinate?'

'Only a little bit,' she confessed with a rueful smile. 'Not very much.'

He groaned. 'Well, don't be now. Get in there and grovel, and only say nice things about your boss. That's me. Remember?' Penny-Rose had never been reluctant to give a bit of cheek, and Bert shook his head at her. 'Know your place, girl, and, short of letting the prince have his wicked way with you, agree to anything. I can always back out later.'

He meant he could always dismiss her, she thought, her laughter fading. If it was a choice of Penny-Rose or the team, it had to be the team.

Maybe she had been too cheeky. Was the aristocracy so sensitive? Heavens, why didn't she learn to keep her mouth shut? Still, if damage had been done, it was she who'd have to undo it.

'If I'm not back in a week, demand entry to the dungeons,' she said, more lightly than she felt. She looked down at her grimy self and thought of what she was facing. 'You really mean go right now?'

'I mean go right now,' Bert said heavily. 'That's what the aristocracy wants, so that's what the aristocracy gets.'

They were waiting.

Penny-Rose walked up through the terraced gardens toward the main castle entrance and found the head gardener waiting. They walked into the courtyard where a butler was waiting in turn. He gave her a wintry smile, turned and led her into the house.

And what a house!

The castle had been built in the twelfth century and maintained by fastidious owners ever since. Castaliae was one of the few countries in the world where the royal family had never deviated from direct succession. It had led to a certain simplicity—the family were the de Castaliaes, the estate was Castaliae and so was the country.

It was confusing maybe, but it certainly must make ordering letterheads easier, Penny-Rose had decided when she'd first learned about the place. And now, looking around the ancestral home of the country's rulers, she saw other advantages of continuous succession. The halls were filled with exquisite furniture, gathered over a thousand years, the walls were hung with fabulous tapestries and the whole place was filled with light and colour from a building designed far in advance of its time.

Every south face had been used to effect— no one here had worried about window taxes— and sunlight streamed in everywhere.

The Castaliae family had been known to sit on the fence for all the castle's history, Penny-Rose knew. The independence of this tiny principality was a tribute to the political savvy of its royal family.

Penny-Rose glanced about her with awe as she was led from room to room. For a twenty-six-year-old Australian, this was new and wonderful indeed. She almost forgot to be nervous.

Almost. She remembered again the moment she entered the great hall.

They were waiting for her.

She knew them by sight. Marguerite, of course. The new prince's elderly mother. She was the woman who'd spoken to her in the garden, and her smile was warm and welcoming.

Then there was Belle. Although it wasn't official, rumour had it that she was engaged to be married to the prince. She was a cold fish, the boys had decided, but it didn't stop them admiring her good points. She might be a cold fish, but she was a very beautiful cold fish.

Belle didn't move from her seat now, and she certainly didn't smile.

And, of course, there was Alastair. Alastair de Castaliae... His Serene Highness, they said, if he could figure out the inheritance hiccups.

And why shouldn't he be the prince? she thought. He certainly had the look of it. He might be dressed for farmwork now, in an ancient pair of moleskins and a shirt that was grubby and frayed at the cuffs, but he was still drop-dead gorgeous, with a smile to die for.

Mmm! He was smiling now—sort of—as he rose to greet her. It was a smile that stilled her nerves and caught her attention as nothing else could. What a smile. And what a...

Well, what a man!

Penny-Rose had never had time to play round with the opposite sex but a lack of time had never stopped her appreciating what was in front of her. And this one was worth appreciating! He was tall, lean and hard-muscled, with long, long legs, and...

And she wasn't a schoolgirl, she reminded herself sharply. She was twenty-six years old, and she had too many responsibilities to be distracted by any man, much less royalty!

So, with an effort, she pulled her attention away from thoughts which were totally out of place. What on earth did they want?

The prince, gorgeous as he was, was looking at her like he wasn't seeing her. Belle was watching her with a calculating expression Penny-Rose didn't like. It was only Marguerite who was smiling as if she meant it.

'Penny-Rose. How lovely. Will you sit down?'

Sit? Good grief! She looked at the plush cream settee and fought a desire to giggle.

'Um…I'm afraid I'd leave a signature,' she said, and received a swift appraising look from Alastair for her pains. 'If it's all right with you, ma'am, I'm just as happy standing. If you'd just tell me what you want, I'll be off before I spread dirt everywhere.'

'But we need to get to know you,' Alastair said, in a voice that sounded as if he didn't believe what he was saying.

Penny-Rose shook her head. She'd hauled off her cap before she'd come inside so her curls bounced around her shoulders and dust floated free. 'You don't need to get to know me, and I'm not dressed for socialising.' OK, she was being blunt but she was at a disadvantage and she didn't like it. Belle was looking at her like she was some sort of interesting insect, and kowtowing to those higher up the aristocratic ladder had never come naturally to Penny-Rose.

'Just for a minute.' Alastair's voice was strained to breaking point, and she cast him an unsure glance. What was wrong with the man?

'My boss can tell you about me,' she said discouragingly. 'Or are you intending to get to know the whole team better?' That made an interesting plan, but it didn't make her smile. She felt more and more like an insect brought in as part of a collection, and she didn't like the feeling one bit.

'No, but—' Marguerite started.

'Let's just tell her what we want,' Alastair said heavily. 'Don't confuse her any further.' His eyes hadn't left Penny-Rose's face, and they didn't leave it now.

He seemed nice, Penny-Rose thought inconsequentially. He also seemed exhausted, strained to the limit, but still very, very nice. His voice was deep and grave and soft, and he sounded as if he was concerned for her.

His English was excellent—well, it would be, as his mother was English. It was only his words that were troubled.

'I'll come to the point,' he told her, speaking slowly as if measuring each word.

'What my mother wishes to know—what we all wish to know—is whether or not you can be persuaded to marry me.'

For a long, long moment nothing stirred. She stared at them in turn, taking in each of their faces. All of them looked...for heaven's sake, they looked as if they were serious!

'You have to be joking,' she said at last, and it was as much as she could do to find her voice. Her words came out a sort of high-pitched squeak. She coughed and tried again. 'I mean...you are joking, right?'

'I'm not joking.' The look of strain on his face intensified. 'Would I joke about something so serious?'

'Yeah, right.' Her eyes narrowed. 'Did you say marry?'

'I said marry.'

'Then you're either having a laugh at my expense or you're all about in the head,' she said bluntly. 'Either way, I don't think I should stay.' She gave them a last wild look. 'I...I'll see myself out, shall I?'

She didn't wait for an answer. She took herself out of the door and out of the castle, without a backward glance.

CHAPTER TWO

THE prince found Penny-Rose an hour later, when she'd been persuaded, against her better judgement, to go back to work. She was sorting stones and Alastair came up behind her so suddenly that she missed a couple of heartbeats.

As before, his voice was deep and soft and calm—as if nothing lay between them at all.

'Why do they call you Penny-Rose? Why not just Penelope or Penny? Or even Rose?'

As a question it was harmless enough, but the situation was ludicrous. She caught her breath, regretted her missed heartbeats—while this man was around she needed all the heartbeats she could get—sat back on her heels and glared.

The fact that his shirt was open at the throat and the sun was shining on the wispy curls on his chest didn't help at all...

Good grief! Cut it out, she told herself. Put your hormones on the back burner!

'Bert says I'm not to fraternise with the upper classes any more,' she said frankly. 'You've had your joke. If you want something else, ask

Bert. Go away.' Already she could see her boss rising from where he'd been working. He'd been disbelieving when she'd told him what had happened, and then he'd been furious.

'It's their idea of a sick joke,' he'd said. 'It's too bad we're not back in England where I can have a word with the union.'

But they weren't back in England. They were in this tiny principality where normal rules didn't apply, and if Bert wanted to keep his team employed he had to bite his tongue and tell her to get on with stone-walling as if nothing had happened.

'They're paying excellent rates, lass,' he'd told her. 'The best. And we've gone to a lot of expense to get over here. We put up with it if we can, for the good of the team, but you're not to go near them again. Just keep working and forget it.'

So she'd agreed. It had been a big thing for Bert to take on a female apprentice, and she wanted to make it as trouble-free for him as possible. But now this creep wouldn't leave her alone.

'Go away,' she said again, and turned back to her stones. She concentrated fiercely on fitting a neat wedge between two blocks and refused to look at him.

Thankfully she heard Bert's heavy footsteps, and then her boss's Yorkshire accent. 'I'd be grateful if you could speak through me if you have anything to say to the workers, sir.' Bert's words were deferential enough, but his tone was pure bulldog.

She risked a glance up, and to her surprise she saw Alastair raking his fingers through his ruffled black hair. It was a gesture that made him seem almost as bewildered as she was.

And it was gesture that suddenly made him seem much less of a prince—and much more human.

And much more...hormone-confusing?

Get back to work, she told herself fiercely, turning back to her ill-fitting stone. Forget your stupid hormones. And don't look again!

'I need to speak to Penny—'

'Penny-Rose isn't speaking to you. She's heard what you have to say and it doesn't make sense. So leave the lass be.'

'I'm not offering her any indecent proposals.'

'If you were, I'd take my team and walk off your land right now,' Bert told him. 'Money or no money. Penny-Rose is a good lass and a damned fine worker, and I won't have her badgered.'

Wow! Under her cap, she felt her ears go pink with pleasure. Praise from Bert was hard to earn, and valued for what it was. She'd worked hard to get this far.

And for Bert to offer to withdraw his team on her behalf... Goodness!

But Alastair was still trying to speak. 'I don't—'

'Look, what is it you want?' Bert said, exasperated. 'You've upset the lass, you've upset me. If you have anything reasonable to say, then say it. Now. In front of Penny-Rose. Clear the air, like. And then we can say no and get on with our work.'

'I hope you won't say no.'

Bert was getting angrier by the minute.

'Well, what is it?'

'As I said, I want to marry Penny-Rose,' Alastair told him, putting his hands up as if to deflect the storm of protest he knew Bert was capable of. 'I want to marry her for a year. As a business proposition. Nothing more.'

The silence went on for several moments. Penny-Rose stayed crouched by her stones. She wouldn't look up but her fingers had ceased even trying to fit her rocks together.

This was crazy.

She left the answering to Bert, because she couldn't think of a thing to say. Even the normally voluble Bert was having trouble.

'Where I'm from,' Bert said at last, in a voice that sounded as if he'd been winded, 'people don't take brides as business propositions. They take brides for life.' His belligerent jaw jutted forward. 'And just the one of them at that. The locals say you're engaged to some woman up in the house. Well, then. You hang onto her and leave our Penny-Rose alone. Bigamy is something I don't hold with and never shall, and if you so much as come near our lass—'

'This isn't bigamy.'

'Look, I don't know what your rules are—'

'I imagine my rules are exactly the same as yours,' Alastair said wearily, and once again his fingers raked his hair. He looked like he was finding this impossible. 'I'm not intending to marry twice. Or...not at once.'

This was getting crazier and crazier.

'What we want here,' Bert said conversationally, and speaking to the world in general, 'is a strait-jacket. Anyone got one?'

Amazingly, it was Penny-Rose who came to the prince's defence. That last gesture of his had got to her. For some reason this didn't seem like someone making indecent propositions. This seemed like a man at the end of his tether.

'Give him a break, Bert.' She rose and shrugged off some dirt. Then she stood back so there was distance—and Bert—between them, but her eyes met Alastair's and held.

And her chin tilted. This was the look she used when she was meeting trouble head on, and she had a feeling she was meeting it now.

This man's trouble.

'Let him say what he wants,' she told her boss. 'He isn't making sense, but we might as well listen.'

The silence stretched out under the afternoon sun, and in the stillness Penny-Rose was aware that Alastair's gaze never left hers. Their eyes were locked, and it was as if there were questions being asked—and answered—without words being spoken.

And whatever the questions were, her answers must have satisfied him because he gave a slight nod, as if he'd come to a final decision. Some of the confusion left his face.

'It could work.'

'What could work?' Bert asked belligerently, and Penny-Rose laid a hand on her boss's arm.

'Let him say.'

And he did. 'I'm serious,' he said at last, his eyes still fixed on hers. 'I don't have a choice. If I don't marry a lady of unimpeachable virtue, this entire estate will be split.'

'I don't understand,' Bert told him.

'It's the terms of the old prince's will,' Alastair said wearily. 'If I don't make such a marriage then the estate will be sold and, no matter how I look at it, there's no way I can buy it. God knows, I've tried every way over the past couple of months, but the thing's impossible. I'd assume the castle itself will go to the government and be opened to the public as a tourist venue, but the acreage around here will be split up.'

Bert frowned, but he wasn't too surprised. He'd heard the rumours. 'And the village?'

'That's the hard part,' Alastair told him. 'It's the reason I'm considering such a marriage. There are over a hundred families living around the estate. All of those homes will have to be sold, and the cousins who stand to inherit stipulate that they'll be sold on the open market.' He paused and gazed around him, over the river banks to the village beyond. 'I guess you've realised by now how desirable this place is?'

It was. The Castaliae estate contained a fairy-tale village built on the cliffs of one of the most picturesque rivers in the world.

But it still wasn't making sense. Bert was still confused.

'So?' Bert demanded.

'So they'll be sold for a fortune,' Alastair said simply. 'We know that. It's already happened to villages like ours that haven't been protected by one landlord. The locals are well enough off, but they're not so wealthy that they can match the prices of city dwellers and overseas interests.'

He sighed, his gaze returning from the far-off village to the girl before him. Now he was talking directly to her. 'If I can't save it, the village will be deserted in winter and filled with wealthy tourists and designer shops in the summer. The locals will have to move away. They can't bear it, and I can't bear it. So I'm asking you, Penny-Rose, to marry me. If you'll have me.'

More silence.

Penny-Rose's gaze didn't waver. She took him in. Not just his amazing good looks, but the grubbiness of his clothes—he wasn't nearly as dirty as she was, but he obviously hadn't had time to change since he'd been out working with his farm manager this morning—the tension of his stance and the dark shadows under his eyes. He looked like a man close to breaking point.

Then, finally, she allowed herself to look around, at the land he was talking of.

This estate went on for ever. The castle itself was built into the cliff overlooking the river, and at the base of the cliff was a tiny village. Penny-Rose was boarding with a family there, and they thought of this man as their landlord.

But this was indeed a fairy-tale village, with its soft sandstone buildings set into the cliffs on the gently flowing river. Alastair was right. Tourists would outbid any villagers for their homes. And if he couldn't bear to have the villagers evicted, she could understand why not.

'It's a stupid clause,' she said at last, and Alastair nodded.

'It is. My uncle put it in place because my cousin was...wild. What it did was to stop Louis marrying at all, and then Louis died just three months after his father.'

'So why don't you just do what Louis did? Not marry?' It seemed a reasonable solution. Surely the gorgeous Belle could be talked into being a mistress only—with so much money at stake!

'I can't inherit unless I marry.'

'But Louis inherited.'

Alastair shook his head, and the impression of weariness intensified. 'Louis never formally inherited, and the cousins started legal action to recover the property. His death forestalled that, and legal opinion is that the estate and the title is now mine—as long as I *do* marry. As long as I do what Louis didn't.'

'And...your Belle's not a lady of virtue?' Bert butted in. He had things in his stride here—almost. His fierce intelligence was working overtime. 'No?'

'Belle's a wonderful woman,' Alastair said quickly. 'But there are...shadows...in her past.'

'I'd imagine there might be.' Bert's team had little time for a woman they'd decided from the first was prone to giving herself airs. On the first few days of working here there'd been a wall collapse on one of the men. Belle had been seen at the window, watching, but hadn't enquired as to the state of Steve's health or even sent down to ask whether she should contact an ambulance.

With Bert carrying a cellphone, her disinterest had been a minor enough offence and hadn't mattered, but it had rankled.

'What...?' Bert said slowly, his eyes moving from Penny-Rose to Alastair and back again. 'What makes you think our lass here is any different? Virtue-wise, that is?'

'Hey!' Penny-Rose said, shocked into comment. 'Can we leave my virtue out of it?'

'Well, that's it. We can't,' Alastair said heavily. 'My mother—'

'I might have known she'd come into it somewhere.' Bert seemed to be almost enjoying himself now. He had the solid workman's view of the aristocracy, and he didn't mind this man's discomfort. 'Now, there's a lady of virtue.'

Marguerite, when she'd heard of the same accident a day later, had been horrified and had sent every possible comfort to Steve. Settled into the local hospital with a broken foot, Steve had appreciated the attention very much indeed, and so had his mates on his behalf.

'My mother's a lady who thinks ahead,' Alastair told them. 'While I've been seeing to the everyday running of the estate and trying to figure out financial ways of saving it, she's been figuring out the only logical way. Which is marrying Penny-Rose. For a year.'

'But—'

'Like I said, it's a business proposition.' Alastair spread his hands. 'I know this sounds intrusive, but my mother had Penny-Rose's background checked. She's employed investigators, and there's now little she doesn't know. In every respect, this is the sort of woman I need.'

He paused, and then said in a softer tone, avoiding Penny-Rose's eye, 'My mother also says she badly needs money.'

It had stopped being even remotely amusing. Penny-Rose's colour mounted to a fiery crimson and she took a step back. *Investigators...* 'My circumstances are none of your business,' she snapped. 'How dare you?'

But Bert was looking back and forth at the pair of them. 'It seems to me the conversation's getting private,' he said.

'It seems to me the conversation is over,' she flung back, and Bert nodded.

'Yeah, OK. But the man's right. You're strapped for cash, girl, and you know it.' It was Bert who organised a huge percentage of her wages to be sent back to Australia. She kept so little for herself that he'd been horrified. 'Maybe it's like the man says—you need to listen to his proposition.' Bert's sunburned face

creased in resigned amusement. 'Now, what I
suggest—'

'Is what you suggested first and send for a
strait-jacket,' she said through gritted teeth, but
Bert shook his head.

'No. The man's got a problem, and it's a real
one. I'm seeing it now. I don't say his solution
will work but you could do worse than to listen
to what he's proposing.' He glanced at his
watch. 'So... It's two o'clock. We knock off at
four. When we do, you go down to the village,
Penny-Rose, get yourself washed and into
something decent, and you...' He turned and
poked a finger into Alastair's chest. 'You take
her out to dinner. Properly. Pick her up at her
lodgings at six and do the thing in style.'

'I don't need—' Alastair started, but Bert
was on a roll.

'You ask a lady to marry you, you do it properly.'

'I don't want—' Penny-Rose tried, but the
stubby finger was pointed at her in turn.

'Give the man a chance. You can always refuse, and that'll be the end of it. You made me
listen to him. Now you do the same. If he bad-
gers you after tonight, he'll answer to me.'

'Bert—'

'No argument,' Bert said. He'd wavered, but now his decision was made. It was time to get on with what he was here for—stone-walling. Everything else was a nuisance. 'That's my final word.' He turned back to Alastair. 'Now, you get back to your castle where you belong and you, girl, get back to sorting your stones. There's to be no more talk of marriage before tonight.'

'Bert, I can't go out with this man.'

'You can,' Bert said heavily, and the amusement was suddenly gone from his voice. 'This is the man who's paying us, girl, and he's in trouble. You made me listen to him. Well, I have. You can put the good of the team before everything for the moment and give him a fair hearing. That's all I ask.'

'And that's all I ask,' Alastair said, his calm brown eyes resting on her face in a message of reassurance.

Which was all very well, she thought wildly as she sent him a savage glance. Reassure all you like.

Marriage!

The man was seriously nuts!

'Six o'clock, then,' he said. 'You're staying with the Berics? I'll collect you there.'

'How do you know where I'm staying?'

'I know all about you.'

'Then you know what I'm about to say to your crazy proposition,' she flung at him. 'No and no and no.'

'Just listen.'

'I'll listen. And then I'll say no.'

CHAPTER THREE

THE man who called for Penny-Rose four hours later was the same man—but only just. Madame Beric opened the front door, quivering in excitement. Penny-Rose didn't blame her. She was waiting in the kitchen, trying not to quiver herself, and when Alastair was ushered in, she failed.

She definitely quivered.

Whew! This was Cinderella stuff. And where was her fairy godmother when she was needed? She'd put on her only dress that was halfway decent—a white sundress with tiny shoulder straps that was more useful for a day off than for a dinner date. She'd washed and brushed her curls until they shone, but that was as much as she'd done.

There wasn't anything else to do. She wore no adornment. How could she? She didn't have any adornment. Or any cosmetics. In fact, her entire outfit was worth peanuts!

Alastair, on the other hand, was wearing a formal suit that must have cost a mint. It was deep black, Italian made and fitted perfectly.

The black was lightened by the brilliance of his crisp, white shirt and the slash of a crimson silk tie. His normally ruffled black curls had been groomed into submission, there was a faint aroma of very expensive aftershave about him and he looked every inch a man of the world.

Unlike Penny-Rose, who had the look of a woman who'd appreciate diving into a small, dark cupboard.

There wasn't a small, dark cupboard available, and Alastair's dark eyes were twinkling in amusement.

Good grief! She could see why Belle wanted him. In fact, she could see why any woman would want him!

'You look beautiful,' he told her, his wide smile taking in her discomfort and reacting with sympathy.

If she could have known it, he was also reacting with truth.

She did look lovely, Alastair acknowledged as he took in her simple appearance. Money made little difference when it came to pure beauty. Her glossy chestnut curls tumbled about her shoulders. Her face glowed with health and humour, her green eyes were edged with tiny, crinkling laughter lines and her diminutive figure was well suited by the simplicity of her dress. She was five feet four and beautiful, whatever she was wearing.

But Penny-Rose couldn't tell what he was thinking, and the thoughts that were whirling around in her head were very different.

She was about as far from his beautiful Belle as any woman was likely to be, she thought bitterly. She wore little make-up, her nose had the temerity to sport freckles, and as for her hands...

Belle's hands would be flawless—of course. They'd be groomed for wearing fabulous jewellery and doing little else. Penny-Rose's hands had been put to hard physical work from the time she could first remember, and it showed.

Alastair reached out for her hand in greeting and she felt him stiffen as he came into contact with the roughened skin. He looked down involuntarily.

Her hands were worn and calloused. They were Cinderella hands, and no fairy godmother could have altered them in time for a date with a handsome prince.

She saw his face change—twist—in a half-mocking smile.

'It is true,' he said slowly, inspecting her fingers in a way that made her attempt to haul her hands out of reach. But he held on, and kept inspecting. 'What my mother said about you is right.'

She was thoroughly flustered, by his words and the feel of her hand in his. 'I have no idea what your mother said,' she snapped, hauling free her fingers. 'But if it's that I have no time for nonsense then, yes, it's the truth. So can we get this dinner over and be done with it?'

'You sound like you aren't looking forward to it.'

'I'm not.'

But, in fact, that was a lie. There were few village families prepared to take in lodgers, so Penny-Rose had had to be grateful for what she'd been able to find. Madame Beric was a kindly enough soul but she was a gifted watercolour artist, with little time for anything else. Her cooking was therefore appalling. Penny-Rose was now up to turnip soup version thirty-four, and burned turnip soup version thirty-four at that...

'Where are we going?' she asked, despite herself, and Alastair's face creased again into one of his blindingly attractive smiles.

'Lilie's, of course,' he said softly. 'Where else does a man take a woman when he's asking her to marry him? It's the best, and tonight only the best will do.'

*   *   *

It was a twenty-minute journey—twenty minutes while Penny-Rose sat in stunned silence in the passenger seat of Alastair's car. A Ferrari. Of course. She'd never been near such a car in her life. Alastair's shabby clothes of earlier had been token workman-like apparel, she thought resentfully. No wonder her hands fascinated him. He wouldn't know what it was to work hard with his hands.

Everything about this man screamed money.

And now he wanted more and he was prepared to marry a stranger to get it.

Maybe that was unfair, she acknowledged. Maybe it was true that he was concerned about the villagers.

She glanced across at him as they pulled to a halt in the restaurant car park, and found that he was twisting to survey her with the same intensity she was using on him. Their gazes met. She flushed and turned away.

'You don't approve of me, do you?' he asked cautiously and she bit her lip.

'I'm not here to make a judgement,' she said at last. 'I'm here because my boss told me to be here.'

'And to eat a wonderful dinner?'

There was that. She had the grace to concede the point and her lips gave an involuntary twitch into a smile. 'Um...OK.'

'My mother says you know what it is to be hungry.'

That comment killed her smiling urge. She returned to glaring, shoved the car door open and then stood and waited for him to get out and lock his damned expensive car.

'I said the wrong thing,' he said ruefully, as they turned toward the restaurant.

'My stomach is my business,' she said with dignity.

'I guess it is.'

She said nothing—just concentrated on where they were going. Damn him, he had her right off balance and she didn't know how to deal with it. Somehow she just had to get this over with. Concentrate on dinner...

Luckily, Lilie's was worth concentration.

The restaurant was built into the parapets of another mediaeval castle. Well, why not? This was fairy-tale country, with castles here to spare.

But there were modern touches. A lift swept them to the rooftop, where the restaurant was situated among the battlements. Floor-to-ceiling windows were now installed where archers had once stood to protect their fortress—and Penny-Rose saw the view and gasped in delight. She'd been trying to disregard Alastair's disturbing presence until now, but the view made her almost forget him.

Almost? Well, almost a little bit…

Focus on the view, she told herself. And what a view! It was as if they were perched in an eagle's nest high over the river. Below were river plains, golden with buttercups and inhabited by placidly grazing cattle. At every turn of the river were more ruins, more castles, and more…

More stone!

'What are you thinking?' Alastair asked, watching her with bemused interest.

'I'm thinking…' she said slowly, and paused.

'Yes?'

'That there's a lifetime of work for me in this country,' she managed, and his eyebrows shot to his hairline.

'What on earth…?'

'Stone-walling,' she breathed. 'Look at it out there—all those stones. All those crumbling walls, just waiting for repair.'

He shook his head. 'I don't believe this.'

'What don't you believe?'

That he'd taken a woman out to dinner—and she was talking about stone?

'Um…stone walls are just stone walls,' he managed, and she gazed at him as if he'd just uttered a profanity.

'That's like saying every house is just a house. And they say you're a well-respected architect. Is that what you believe?'

'I… No.' He was flummoxed. This woman was like no woman he'd ever dated.

'Well, there you go, then.' She smirked. 'I rest my case.'

He grinned. They were being led to a discreet table tucked into a niche where all they had for company was the view. 'OK,' he conceded. 'But…'

'But?'

'I never thought I'd be wining and dining a woman who'd look at rock and gasp.'

She gave him a look of gentle mockery. 'Surely not. You must be using the wrong rock. Have you tried diamonds?'

He cast her an amused glance—she certainly was different—but then was distracted by the need to order champagne.

Penny-Rose didn't protest. She could count the times she'd tasted champagne on one finger. She cast another long look out over the valley,

she gazed around her again at the opulent restaurant setting—and she decided there and then
that she wasn't about to let scruples get in the
way of a very good dinner.

And Alastair saw it. 'You're intending to
milk this for everything it's worth,' he said
dryly, and she had the grace to blush.

'Um…yes.'

'Because?'

'Because I shouldn't be here. I have no intention of agreeing to any crazy marriage pro-
posal but, as you say, I've been hungry.' She
beamed, abandoning herself to enjoyment, and
gave a small bounce on the beautifully padded
chair. 'Wow. This looks like a very nice place
to eat.'

He was fascinated. She'd bounced. She'd definitely bounced.

'What?' she demanded, seeing his expression. 'What did I do wrong?'

'Nothing.'

'I just said it looks a great place to eat.'

He took a deep breath. 'That, Miss O'Shea,
is an understatement. Can I interest you in some
snails?'

'You can interest me in anything that's not
turnip soup,' she said, and received another
startled look. 'That's what the Berics live on,'

she explained. She shook her head. 'Every night, M'sieur Beric sits down to turnip soup, and every night he finishes it, looks up and tells his wife it was delicious. So she makes it the next night. And if she doesn't, he gets all disappointed.' She grinned. 'So you see why I finally agreed to eat with you?'

'Despite disapproving of me?'

Her smile widened. 'Despite that.'

He paused, but he had to ask. 'Why?'

'Why what?

'Why do you disapprove of me?'

'Because you're a prince and I'm a worker,' she said frankly. 'Cinderella was a fairy story. It doesn't happen in real life.'

'It might.'

'Oh, yeah?' It was a gentle jeer. 'Even Cinderella's prince didn't propose marriage just for a year!'

Alastair thought that through and disagreed. 'Her guy had his deadlines, too,' he told her, semi-seriously. 'Like midnight. Seeing carriages turn to pumpkins just as the going gets romantic might put a man right off his stride.'

'I'd imagine it might,' she said faintly.

'So Cinderella's beloved had to work fast.' He paused again, and then his smile died. 'As I do.'

'If you want to be Prince.'

'No.' Alastair shook his head.

The champagne arrived. There was a moment's silence while the bubbles were poured, and he waited until she'd taken her first gorgeous sip. He waited for her verdict, and he got it.

'Yum!' she said, and he smiled at her pleasure. *Yum.* It was a word Belle hadn't used in her life!

But he couldn't afford to be distracted by this strange Cinderella his mother had found for him. He had this one meal to persuade her, and he already knew persuasion would take some doing.

'I really don't want to be a prince,' he said, and his eyes met hers over the glass. 'Will you believe that?'

'Um...' She took another cautious sip and made her decision. 'No.'

He had to make her believe. Otherwise nothing would make sense. 'Fame,' he said slowly, 'isn't all it's cracked up to be. This principality is small, but as the eldest—indeed, only—male of the royal family, the spotlight is now on me. There's a population of a tiny country waiting to see what I do.'

He motioned out the window to the tiny holdings scattered along the river. 'There are so many families whose lives depend on my choice—and your choice, too.'

'Don't you dare try to blackmail me,' she snapped, suddenly angry, and his expression softened.

'No. I won't. But according to my mother, our needs mesh.'

She glared some more. 'I don't understand.'

'A year as my wife would set you up for life.'

'I don't need to be set up—'

'You can barely afford to eat now,' he pointed out. 'Michael is still at secondary school and he wants to be an engineer. How are you going to afford three of them at university?'

She placed her champagne glass carefully down on the table. All of a sudden the bubbles tasted like vinegar.

'You really have pried...'

'My mother has on my behalf.' His calm gaze met hers, and his hands reached out across the table and took hers. She didn't pull back. He looked down at those work-worn hands, and his mouth twisted into the mocking smile she was starting to know well.

'You want a résumé of all my mother found out about you?'

'No, I—'

'Because I intend to give it to you.' He shook his head at her indignant protest, released her hands and sat back, assessing. His eyes rested on hers, like she was an enigma he was still trying to figure out.

'Your mother was an invalid,' he started, watching her face. 'She had multiple sclerosis. She should never have had one child, let alone four, but your father was desperate for a son. After three daughters, she finally died giving birth to Michael. That was when you were ten.'

'I don't—'

'I'm saying this no matter how much you interrupt,' he continued. 'So you may as well listen and make sure I have it right. We wouldn't like to make any mistakes here.'

'Of course not,' she said bitterly, and Alastair smiled.

'Very wise. So what did you have? A father who's a farmer and an expert stone-waller, but who coped with his wife's illness by turning to the bottle.' He held his hand up as Penny-Rose made an involuntary protest and she subsided. Reluctantly. 'And a mother who depended on her eldest daughter for everything.

'And then your mother died.' His voice softened still further. 'Which left you at ten, caring for Heather, six, Elizabeth, four and Michael who was newborn. And a herd of dairy cows and a father who drank himself stupid every night, leaving everything else to you.'

'I don't—'

'Welfare nearly stepped in,' he went on. 'The whole district was concerned. My mother's investigators had no trouble finding people who remembered gossip about your family. I gather you came within an inch of being put into care. But for you.'

'I didn't—'

But he was brooking no interruptions. Like Cinderella's prince, he was working to a deadline. 'You worked your butt off,' he told her. 'You came home from school every night and you milked. You got up at dawn and did the same. The neighbours knew and were horrified but you wouldn't have it any other way, and when Welfare tried to step in they were met by a little girl whose temper matched that of any adult. ''Leave us alone,'' you said. ''We'll survive.'' And somehow you did, until you could leave school at fifteen and work full time on the farm.'

'Yes, but—'

'But it wasn't much easier then, was it, Penny-Rose?' he said gently. 'Because your father drank any profits, and you had your work cut out keeping bread on the table. When your father got drunk one night and smashed his car into a tree, things might have been easier. If the younger children had left school. But you wouldn't let them.'

'Of course not. They're so clever,' she said desperately. 'All of them. Heather wants so much to be a doctor. Like you, Elizabeth wants architecture.' She flashed him a wintry smile. 'And somehow you already know that Michael longs for engineering.'

'You're supporting two at university now and one at school. How are you going to do more?'

'They have part-time jobs. They help.'

'Not enough. It's two more years until Heather finishes and Michael's major expenses haven't started. You're up to your ears in debt already.'

'I don't need to listen to this!'

'No, but you should,' Alastair said ruthlessly. 'You can't do it. You've come to Europe because the pay's better. With a great exchange rate you can send more money home, but there's an end to it. You can't stretch your debts any further.'

'I must,' she said in a small voice, and his hand came back across the table and caught hers.

'You need a life, too.'

'They're great kids.' Her green eyes sparked with anger. 'We've talked it through. As soon as Michael's finished, it's my turn. That's when I can start enjoying myself.'

'Oh, great. In six years? More! How much more turnip soup, Penny-Rose? How long before they're self-supporting and you have your debts paid off?'

'I want them to have the best,' she said stubbornly. 'They shouldn't suffer because my father...'

'Because your father didn't face his responsibilities.' Alastair's voice gentled. 'You face yours, though, don't you? And I do, too. That's what this is all about. Facing responsibilities. That's why I'm asking you to marry me. It could help us both.'

'I don't—'

'No, don't say anything.' He smiled at her, a smile that lit his face and took the heaviness away from her heart. 'First let's eat a very good dinner. And tell me...'

'Tell you what?' She was thoroughly flustered. 'You already know everything.'

'I don't know this.'

'What?'

'Why do they call you Penny-Rose?'

She didn't answer him until she'd demolished the first course. Her snails were magnificent morsels of taste sensation. She'd never tasted anything so delicious in her life. And in a way, it was time out. Her whole attention had to be on conquering the tricky silver tongs and tiny fork—and on not missing a drop of the gorgeous juice.

She finally finished and looked up to find Alastair watching her. The look on his face was strange, as if he couldn't believe she was real.

'Oh, what?' she said crossly. 'Have I made a *faux pas*?'

'On the contrary, you managed beautifully,' he told her, just a hint of a smile lingering in his voice. 'In fact, I don't think I've ever enjoyed watching someone eating snails more.' He left her to make of that what she liked, and then pressed home his question for the third time. 'Before our next distraction comes—'

'Food's not a distraction,' she retorted. 'What a thing to say!'

'OK, I was brought up wrong,' he admitted. 'I could have had snails for breakfast if I'd wanted. But I do want to know—'

'You know everything.'

'Not this.'

'So pay more money to your private investigators.'

'My mother asked them,' he confessed. 'But apart from knowing your full name is Penelope Rose O'Shea...'

'So? That's why I'm called Penny-Rose.'

'No.' He shook his head. 'It'd explain Penny, or Rose, but—'

'I hate Penny.'

Alastair's face was thoughtful, watching hers. 'I see you do. Why don't you call yourself Penelope, then?'

'I'm not much into that either.'

'Would you like to explain?'

'My...' She caught herself. No! This was none of his business. It was no one's business.

But then she looked at him again, and he looked gravely back, and she thought, He *does* want to know. For whatever reason, he's really interested.

In me.

The thought was so novel she could hardly believe it. Talking about herself was something she never did, but suddenly she couldn't resist telling him. Just once.

'My father called me Penelope,' she began. 'He insisted I was called that after a great-aunt, so she'd leave us money. But she never did, and my father hated the name because of it. And I think…' She took a deep breath. 'I think my father hated me.'

'That's a fair indictment of your father.'

She shook her head. 'Maybe I don't blame him. I was his conscience, you see,' she told him. 'From the time my mother died I badgered him. All Dad wanted was to drink himself into oblivion, and I wouldn't let him.'

'How did you stop him?'

She shrugged. 'It was never easy. I'd steal money from his wallet to feed the kids, so when he went to the pub he didn't have enough. A great little thief—that's me. Or I'd wake him up sometimes…' Her voice faltered as she tried to continue. 'When I was ill or when the milking got too much for me, I'd sometimes be able to shame him into helping. And I badgered him into teaching me to build stone fences. He had to work a bit to get money to drink, so he'd take on a stone-walling job, and there I'd be, watching. Because it meant money, I'd help all I could.'

'I'd have thought,' Alastair said thoughtfully, his eyes resting on hers, 'that he'd have been grateful.'

'He wasn't.' There was no question of that. 'He called me Penelope. He'd put on this dreadful voice and he'd say to the kids, "Penelope says we have to do this. Penelope says there's not enough to eat…"' She broke off. 'He'd tell the kids it was my fault they were hungry—because I'd taken his money! Sometimes it was as if I had another kid to look after, but he was my father. I couldn't stop him hating me. The only way I could get through to him was to threaten to come into the pub and tell his drinking mates how much we'd had to eat that week.'

'You didn't!' Alastair said, awed, and she managed a smile.

'You have no idea what you can do when you're desperate. Only then…after the first time I threatened that, he started calling me Penny instead of Penelope. He said I was constantly grubbing for money so I might as well be named for it. I hated that, too. So, behind his back, the kids started calling me Penny-Rose.'

'I see…'

'And it's sort of stuck,' she told him. 'And maybe it fits me. Penelope Rose is on my passport and job application, but when I got the job with Bert they said I was such a two-bit thing they'd call me Penny-Rose.' She smiled. ''Cos I surely wasn't a two-bob Rose.'

There was silence as he took that on board. The waiter came and cleared their plates, but still Alastair didn't speak.

'I don't think you're a two-bob Rose either,' he said at last, and he couldn't quite keep the emotion out of his voice. He looked at her across the table and he couldn't believe what he was seeing. All this... His mother had told him her background, but until now it had hardly seemed true.

'I don't think you're a two-bob Rose either,' he repeated. 'I refuse to call you Penny. Or Penelope. I think you're a Rose, and a million-pound Rose at that. A Princess Rose. You deserve it, and marriage to me might just make sure that you get it. From this time on...' His voice caught with sudden, unexpected emotion. 'From this time on, you're Rose.'

'Rose...'

'Don't you like it?'

'Yeah, but it doesn't sound like me.' She grinned. 'It sounds too dignified.'

'You can live up to your name.'

'Yeah, right.'

'If you want to...'

The main course arrived then, giving them welcome time out. Penny-Rose—or just Rose—was never going to be distracted from food like this, not for all the princes in the world.

Before her was roast duckling, snow peas and crispy roast potatoes, served with a *jus* that made her mouth water before she even saw it. Penny-Rose-cum-Rose forgot all about dignity and concentrated on what was important.

Which was a novelty in itself to Alastair. He wasn't accustomed to taking a woman out to dinner and having all her attention focussed on the food!

He sat and watched, bemused, waiting for the moment when she'd scraped her plate clean, and then turned back to more mundane questions. Like marriage proposals.

She turned straight back to practicalities.

'I can see you have a problem marrying Belle,' she said at last, popping a final snow pea into her mouth and savouring it with regret that it was the last. 'But why did you choose me as an alternative? I'd imagine there must be lots of nice, virtuous girls in your principality.'

'Um, yes.' He seemed discomfited and she pressed home her point.

'So why did you choose to investigate my background?'

'You were my mother's choice.'

'Oh, right. And you always do what your mother tells you?'

He grinned. 'Always.'

'Why don't I believe you?'

'In this instance I think she's done very well.'

'But why me?' she pressed again.

He hesitated, but decided he might as well be honest. 'Because you're Australian.'

She frowned at that. 'You'll have to explain.'

'At the end of our marriage,' he told her, playing with the cutlery still lying on the table, 'you'll need to walk away. I don't want television and newspapermen in your face for the rest of your life. I'd imagine you don't want that either.'

'No,' she said, startled.

'This marriage will create publicity.' He paused. 'You know I've been engaged to be married before?'

'I did know that,' she said, a trace of sympathy entering her voice. This man stood to inherit the rulership of this tiny country and you couldn't cross the border without hearing the gossip. 'Her name was Lissa and she was killed in a car crash three years ago.'

'With my father.'

'I'd heard that as well.' Her face softened still further. 'I'm sorry.'

He shrugged off her sympathy. He didn't need it. He just needed to make her see why it mattered. 'Then maybe you'll understand why I don't want to get emotionally involved again.'

'Hence Belle.' She nodded wisely, thinking of what the gossip columnists said about Alastair's companion. 'I can see that, too.'

He heard the gentle criticism—the same concern that came from his mother when she asked whether he was sure he was doing the right thing—and it stung. 'Belle will make me a very good wife.'

'I'm sure she will.'

His eyes narrowed, but Penny-Rose's face was cordiality itself.

'Apart from the virtue bit,' she added. 'That's hard. To be hit now for flings you had in your youth. So...' She cocked her head. 'You're not in love with Belle?'

'I'm not in love with anyone.'

'No?' She was like a brightly inquisitive sparrow, he thought, impossible to take offence at. But she was insistent. She was still waiting.

'No. I'm not in love with anyone,' he repeated stiffly. 'After Lissa, it's impossible.'

'Lissa was some lady?'

'We were second cousins and we grew up together,' he told her, his voice softening. 'We were the best of friends.'

He received a probing look as Penny-Rose thought this through. 'So... You're thirty-two now, and you didn't get engaged until three years ago. They say you'd only just become engaged when she was killed. And you and Lissa were friends for years.' She paused and thought it through some more. 'Then after years of friendship, passion suddenly overtook you so you decided to marry?'

He frowned at that, and fingered his wineglass, sending shards of candlelight glistening through the Burgundy. 'Aged almost thirty, we realised how good friendship could be.'

'So you weren't in love with Lissa either?'

His face darkened. 'I loved Lissa.' And from the way he'd said it, she was sure it was the truth. But maybe he hadn't loved her as a man could love a woman. Or...as she'd always hoped a man could love a woman.

For heaven's sake... What would she know? she thought suddenly. Maybe what she was thinking of was a romantic dream. It was a dream she'd always had at the back of her mind, but still just a dream for all that.

She could hardly probe any further down that road, but there was still something not quite right. She sipped her wine and wrinkled her freckled nose. 'And Belle?' she pressed. 'She's a friend, too?'

'Not like Lissa was, but...' Alastair hesitated, but this was a major commitment he was asking of this woman, and it was important for him to be honest. He knew that. If she agreed, she had to know exactly what she was letting herself in for. 'Belle's an interior decorator—a partner with my Paris architectural firm. She knows what I expect in a woman, she entertains my clients magnificently and she doesn't interfere with my need for privacy.'

'Your need for privacy! That's a wonderful basis for a marriage—I don't think.' Her words were out before she could hide the revulsion in her voice, and he heard it. His brows snapped down in anger.

'Privacy and mutual support is all either Belle or I need.'

'I...I understand.' Penny-Rose did, too, and the thought made a shudder run down her spine. He saw, and his frown deepened even further.

'You're cold?'

'How could I be cold?' It was the most beautiful spring evening. But his concern was warming, she thought. Nice.

'So let me get this right,' she continued. 'You want me to play the fairy-tale princess for a year, then at the end of it to calmly apply for a divorce, hitch up my socks and walk out of here. Leaving you to Belle.'

'I wouldn't have put it quite like that but, yes. That sums it up.'

'And Belle?' Penny-Rose toyed with her wineglass. 'How does she feel about it? If it were me,' she said carefully, 'I wouldn't be happy about seeing my fiancé marry someone else first. In fact,' she added honestly, 'it'd be pistols at dawn if anyone made the attempt.'

He smiled at the image. 'That's hardly sensible. And Belle's sensible. I told you. She understands that the needs of the country have to come first.'

'I see.' Or she saw enough to make her shiver again.

But she needed to concentrate on her own role. Not Belle's future one. 'Is this really going to be OK?' she asked. 'Will the lawyers be happy with a twelve-month marriage?'

'The inheritance doesn't say how long I have to stay married. Legal opinion is that if the marriage doesn't last a year then annulment rather than divorce could be considered and it could risk the inheritance. But if it lasts a year—'

'Then you and Belle can be safe as Prince and Princess and live happily ever after.' She nodded wisely—but there was something else niggling her. Something else that needed asking, and there was no easy way to ask it.

'Um…how do you know I'm unimpeachably virtuous?' she demanded.

He looked across at her, startled, and then he grinned. 'The investigators say you've never had a boyfriend. According to my mother, you haven't had time.'

'Gee, thanks.'

'It does make things easier,' he told her. 'And your maturity helps. If I marry a woman who's not mature then I risk her falling…'

'Falling for you?'

'There's not much chance of that happening,' he said bluntly. 'Not with the way I feel about marriage. But falling for the trappings of the position.'

'What makes you think I won't?'

'You're a pragmatist,' he replied. 'My mother says so, and I'm starting to accept that she's right. You do what you need to do to survive.' He grinned again. 'Besides, you're

Australian. If the worst comes to the worst, after twelve months I can kick you out of the country. But I don't think I'll need to do that. You'll be wanting to get back to your sisters and brother. And you'll have your fee.'

Now they were getting down to business. 'My fee,' she said faintly.

The thought suddenly seemed repugnant. But... According to Alastair and his mother, she was a pragmatist. So she'd just better school her features into interest and behave like one. A virtuous pragmatist.

It sounded like something to take for constipation. Or... She grinned. Maybe it sounded more like someone who played very boring music!

Get a grip, she told herself. Was it the champagne that was going to her head? 'What...what exactly were you thinking of as a fee?' she asked unsteadily, and he nodded as if he'd expected the question.

He was certainly prepared—and then some! 'My accountant suggests an allowance of ten thousand English pounds per week, over and above expenses, for the entire time we're married, and a further one million pounds settlement at the time of the divorce.'

She'd raised her wineglass to her lips, she'd taken a sip—but the wine didn't go down. She choked and choked again, and finally Alastair came around to thump her shoulders.

The feel of his hand on the bare skin of her back did nothing at all to help her composure. By the time she'd finished coughing she was bright pink and thoroughly flustered.

'I'm sorry,' she gasped at last. 'I thought you said...a million pounds!'

'I did. Plus the rest.'

'That's ridiculous.' She was almost angry.

'No. I'm rich already. I might not have enough to buy the estate at the values tourists would put on it, but if I inherit, I'll have more money than I know what to do with. My lawyers say that if I'm not generous, I could face a lawsuit later. I don't want that. And my mother says you deserve this windfall, and I'm starting to believe that she's right.'

'And...' She still couldn't take it in. 'Belle agrees to it?'

'Belle's the woman I want with me long term,' he said slowly. 'After losing Lissa, I don't want anyone or anything making emotional demands. Belle's a wonderful partner and she understands—'

'She understands what little you want of her.' Penny-Rose nodded, though the thought of the marriage he was contemplating made her feel dreadful. 'And she understands me?'

'She sees you as a necessary evil.'

'Gee, thanks.'

'Say nothing of it.' He smiled, his dangerous, coaxing smile that had her half-inclined to agree just so she could see it once more. He was still standing, looking down at her, and his very closeness was unnerving.

The whole situation was unnerving.

And there were things she didn't understand. Lots of things.

'I'd imagine, as a prince, yours would be a very public wedding,' she said slowly.

'Yes. It'll need to be.'

'Then how will your people take it?' she went on, thinking it through as she spoke, 'when I disappear after twelve months?'

'My people are pragmatists,' he said. 'Like yourself. There's discontent now because the succession is at risk. Even though my engagement to Belle hasn't been official, the gossip columnists have voiced rumours and disapprove. They know about the inheritance, and they want the principality to continue. Our marriage will dispel that worry.'

But she was no longer listening. She'd been caught by a word. A very major word. Succession... She almost choked again.

'Hey, you don't want me to have a baby, do you?' she demanded, and Alastair smiled. Drat! How could she concentrate when he smiled like that? But she *must* concentrate. 'There's no stipulation about babies in the old prince's will?'

And now he was laughing at her. 'No. I think Belle and I can manage that. Eventually.'

'That fits in the category of what an elegant hostess does?' Penny-Rose enquired politely, and his smile faded.

'There's no need—'

'To be impertinent?' Her equilibrium almost restored, she managed a chuckle as Alastair finally sank down again into his chair. 'I'm sorry but I'm always impertinent. You should know that if you intend marrying me.'

'Then you will marry me?'

She put up a hand. 'I'm thinking about it. Nothing more.'

'That's all I ask.'

'How long do I have to make up my mind?'

'Until coffee,' he told her, and her equilibrium disappeared all over again.

'Help...'

'If you don't agree, I need to find someone else,' he said apologetically. 'And pragmatic single women of unimpeachable virtue…'

'Are a bit thin on the ground?' Penny-Rose was fighting for composure. 'I guess you could always put an advertisement in the international press. WANTED: PRINCESS FOR A YEAR. I imagine you'd be swamped by callers.'

'Maybe I would be.' He smiled faintly. 'But I can't do that.'

'Why not?'

'This marriage,' he said slowly, 'has to appear real.'

'To appease the cousins?'

'And the lawyers. That's right.'

'But…' She thought this through. 'Bert and the team already know it'd be a marriage of convenience.'

He shrugged. 'A marriage of convenience doesn't necessarily mean it's not a real marriage. Royal marriages have been just that for thousands of years. But advertising seems a bit over the top, and I can't publicly stipulate a time frame. I'm running a fine legal line.'

'You certainly are.' She glanced up at him and then away again. He was starting to disconcert her. He was speaking of business. He was planning out his whole life—first with her and then Belle—as if he was planning a commercial venture.

The thought left her feeling almost ill.

What a waste, she thought suddenly. Arranged marriages might be what was expected of royalty, but... With Alastair's wonderful smile, and his caring nature—and his money and his castle...

He was some catch!

He was some prince!

That wasn't the way to think, she told herself hastily. Alastair was planning this as a business proposition, and so must she.

'A million pounds,' she murmured, forcing her thoughts sideways and letting herself dwell on what that could mean. 'A million... Do you have any idea how tempting that sort of money is for a girl like me?'

'I can imagine.' Alastair smiled at her across the table and she had to give herself the same business-only lecture she'd given herself thirty seconds ago. It was either that or go take a cold shower. But he didn't seem to notice. Maybe he had that effect on all women! 'You'd never have to work again,' he was saying.

His words startled her, breaking through her fog of masculine awareness. Of Alastair awareness… 'Not work?' Penny-Rose frowned. 'I wouldn't know how to not work.'

'You could learn,' he said gently, 'during your year as a princess.'

'Oh, right. Just swan around, adjusting my tiara and polishing my throne. I don't think so.'

'You'd be a figurehead…'

'A figurehead who still has to get herself a master stone-waller certificate. I'm not going home without it.'

He stared at her. 'You won't need to stone-wall. A million pounds will set you up for life.'

She looked blankly at him, as if he were speaking some foreign language. 'But I *like* stone-walling.'

'You couldn't possibly stone-wall as my wife.'

'If you stuck me in a castle on a velvet cushion I'd go into a decline,' she said. And then she chuckled. 'Or I'd cause trouble. I just know I would. I'd be sticking my nose into all sorts of things that don't concern me. You need to accept me as a stone-walling bride or not at all.'

Wordless, he sat back and stared some more. Finally he reached across and lifted her fingers again, gazing down at her callouses and scratches left from the day's work. 'You don't want to leave all this?'

'A stone-waller is what I am,' she said simply. She took a deep breath, trying to make him see. 'Alastair, money would be very nice—because of my sisters and my brother—but at the end of the year I've no intention of becoming your pensioner for the rest of my life.'

'There's a lot of women who'd jump at the chance.'

'I'm not a lot of women.'

'I can see that.' He laid her hand down on the table. 'But…if you don't agree to marry me, there's many families here who'll lose their homes.'

'That's the only reason I'm listening.'

'We could make it work.'

Penny-Rose hesitated. 'You'd want a fairy-tale wedding? Lace and chariots and archbishops and the whole catastrophe?'

'Maybe not archbishops. If we're making vows we don't intend to keep, I'd prefer not to do it in a church. The church here is tiny so that can be our excuse. But otherwise, yes, pretty much the whole catastrophe.' And he sounded suddenly as unsure as she felt. They were hurtling into this together and in truth it scared them both.

She stared at him, and she saw his uncertainty—and his need. For some reason, his hesitancy reassured her.

As did his decision not to use a church.

His scruples were the same as hers.

'You'd have to fly my sisters and brother over to watch,' she told him slowly, and for the first time she sounded as if she was starting to think of this marriage as a serious possibility. 'They'd never forgive me if I didn't include them, and if they don't see it for themselves they'll never believe it's real.'

Alastair didn't hesitate. 'I can do that. Of course.'

'And...' She bit her lip, stared at the table for a while and then raised her eyes to meet his. There was something else she had to be sure of, and this was major. 'It really is business only? You wouldn't come near me? As a wife, I mean.' Her face turned pink. 'Um...there'd be separate bedrooms?'

'There are royal precedents for such arrangements.' He grinned, relaxing a little. 'The marriage suite in the castle is two bedrooms with a dressing room in between.'

'How very romantic. And locked doors?'

'Of course,' he said gravely. 'Because you're a lady of unimpeachable virtue.'

'I'm not infringing on Belle's domain.' Her mind was working in overdrive. This was going to be hard, but it had to be said.

'Speaking of Belle... Alastair, she'll have to go.' She hesitated, trying to think of an alternative, but there wasn't one. With Belle included in the arrangement, the marriage idea was preposterous. 'For the full twelve months of our marriage, Belle will need to stay away from the castle. I can't play the part of your wife if you have a mistress in the same house. I'd feel like Belle was watching me, daggers drawn, for the whole year. I'd hate it. She'd hate it. So...' Her troubled eyes managed a twinkle. 'I need to put my wifely foot down.'

Alastair thought that through. It was a reasonable request. Sort of. Belle would resent it, he thought, but on reflection Penny-Rose was right. The whole sham marriage could well founder if she stayed.

Finally he nodded. 'Agreed.'

'And I can keep on stone-walling with Bert?'

That wasn't as easy. 'That'll raise eyebrows. Princesses don't stone-wall.'

'This one does,' she told him. 'Or it's no deal. I'll be your part-time princess and you can be my part-time prince. But from eight to four, it's off with the tiara and on with the overalls.

You can lock the gates so there's nobody to see me do it, apart from Bert and the guys. Bert already knows what the deal is. He'll keep his mouth shut and the men think I'm eccentric anyway.'

'You can't keep stone-walling,' he said faintly, looking again at her hands. 'You can't want to.'

'I can and I do.' She leaned forward, trying to make him understand. 'Alastair, will you continue to be an architect as well as a prince?'

That was different. 'Yes, but—'

'But nothing. I've spent years learning how to stone-wall. I'm good at what I do and it took years of negotiating before I got Bert to employ me. He's giving me the chance of being a master waller. I'm not about to give that chance up now.'

'With the money you'll earn, you won't need to be a master waller.'

'Like you won't need to be an architect. But you won't stop.'

'But—'

Penny-Rose shook her head, refusing to be swayed. 'But nothing. There's no negotiating on this one. I can use your money for the kids' education, and I can't tell you how much of a relief that will be, but afterwards I'll put what remains into a nice little pension plan for when my fingers get too feeble to wiggle copestones.'

'It'll be some pension plan.'

'And very nice it'll be, too.' She chuckled, and her green eyes met his and held. 'You are serious about all this?'

There was only one reply to that. Alastair had no choice. 'I am serious.'

'But…you do have reservations?'

And he had to be truthful again. 'I do.'

'Well, so have I,' she told him. 'But if the choice is for Michael not to go to university and for your villagers to lose their homes, I think we could give it a crack, don't you?'

There was a moment's pause. The thing hung in the air between them—a weighty decision, to be made one way or another right now. Because, marriage of convenience or not, they both knew this decision would change their lives for ever.

But he couldn't step back now. Not when so much was at stake.

'I believe we can give it a crack,' he said at last, and finally he allowed himself to relax. He smiled. 'After dessert, of course. Can I interest you in Pierre's excellent raspberry soufflé?'

'You can indeed,' she said cordially. 'And then let's plan how we intend to get married.'

CHAPTER FOUR

IT WAS amazing how quickly, once a decision had been made, that plans were set in concrete. Before she could change her mind, Alastair told Marguerite and Belle, and Penny-Rose was left to tell Bert.

'One wisecrack about romance and you're dead,' she told her boss. 'It's a marriage of convenience for a year, but the world—and the team—has to think it's indefinite. You know why I'm doing it, and it was you who made me listen to the man. So you can just shut up and support me. Or else.'

Bert did. Surprisingly, he met her decision with wholehearted approval, and proceeded to tell the men—confidentially—that Penny-Rose was taking a step up in the world. He didn't tell them about the time frame, but he did tell them everything else.

The men sat in stunned silence while they took it in.

And then they wholeheartedly approved! In the time they'd worked with her, the team had become extraordinarily fond of their 'Penny-

Rose', and in their opinion her stroke of good fortune couldn't have happened to anyone nicer.

But they couldn't understand why she was still sorting rocks as if nothing had happened.

'I'm not royal yet,' she retorted. 'And even when I'm married, I'll still be me.' Still Penny-Rose, she thought. Not Rose yet. 'I'm better off out here.'

Out of the publicity, she meant. Here, in the secluded castle grounds, working alongside her friends, she was shielded from media hype. She could concentrate on what she was good at and block out her increasing nervousness.

She could also block out her siblings' reactions. Which was tricky.

Because she couldn't tell them it was a business arrangement which would last only for a year. They felt so indebted to her already... If they knew she was doing this for them, she'd have a mass educational walk-out, which was the last thing she wanted.

So she told Heather the bare facts and left her sister to fill in the gaps as best she could. Which Heather did, with relish.

'That's just fantastic.' Heather could hardly believe it. 'Oh, Penny-Rose, I always knew

you'd marry someone special. A real live
prince? Is he fabulous?'

'I guess you could call him fabulous,' she
said cautiously, and Heather chuckled.

'He'd have to be if you've decided to marry
him. I know what you think of marriage.' She
hesitated and Penny-Rose could hear her uncertainty down the line. 'What does he call
you? Penelope?'

'Rose.'

'Even though he knows you're called
Penelope?'

'Yes.'

'You'll be Princess Rose?'

'I guess so.' She took a deep breath. 'He
says...he says he won't call me Penny-Rose because I'm worth much more.' She didn't add
that the way he called her Rose made her feel
odd—like he was deliberately distancing himself from who she really was.

But Heather loved it. 'Then he is special,'
Heather said soundly. 'And...' Penny-Rose
could imagine her sister's glee on the other end
of the line. 'Is he very rich?'

'Um, yes.'

'Specialler and specialler.'

Penny-Rose grinned. 'Specialler... Is that
good grammar?'

'Always the big sister. Leave my grammar alone. When do we get to meet him?'

'The wedding's in six weeks. Alastair will send you plane tickets, if you can come.'

There was a squeal of delight from the other end of the phone. 'Really?'

'Really.'

'Oh...' A long sigh of pure pleasure. 'Try and keep us away. Can we be bridesmaids?'

'I'm not having bridesmaids.'

'Princesses always have bridesmaids.'

'Not this one.'

'But...' There was a slight pause. 'It is going to be a royal wedding—right?'

There was only one answer to that. 'Yes.'

'Fabulous.' Another sigh, then... 'Help, we don't have anything to wear.'

This had already been discussed. 'Alastair's sending you a cheque,' she told her sister. 'So...so you can get something wonderful to wear.' When she revealed how much the cheque would be for, there was a moment's silence.

'Is this guy for real?'

'Yes.'

'Does he have any brothers?'

That brought another grin. 'No.'

'He must be wonderful,' Heather said at last, when she'd caught her breath. 'It'd take a special sort of prince to look at you in your disgusting work clothes and see the gorgeous Penny-Rose underneath.' She sighed once more. 'You'll be able to stop stone-walling.'

'If anyone asked you to marry him,' Rose said carefully, 'would you stop wanting to be a doctor?'

That halted her sister's romanticism in its tracks. 'Um, no.'

'Then leave my career alone.'

'Alastair's happy for you to stay a stone-waller?'

'It's what I am.'

There was a long, thoughtful silence, and then a sigh so deep it was almost a blessing.

'Oh, Penny-Rose. Oh, love, I'm so happy for you I'm starting to cry.'

There was nothing Penny-Rose could do to prevent her siblings' reactions.

There was also nothing she could do to stop the media frenzy. Even though no formal announcement had been made, their evening at Lilie's had been noticed.

'Stay at the castle from now on,' Alastair told her, and she had no choice. Photographers were camped out at the castle gates. Their night at Lilie's, along with Belle's hasty departure, had been noticed and put together with glee. The media knew how urgently Alastair needed a bride, and Penny-Rose was obviously it.

And she didn't like the sensation at all. The conversion of Penny-Rose to Rose...

'I'm beginning to feel like a poor little rich girl,' she said as she sat down to dinner with Marguerite and Alastair two days later. Reluctantly, she'd moved into the castle guest quarters. At knock-off time she therefore bathed away her grime and presented herself at the dinner table as a normal guest.

A normal guest? Ha! She didn't feel in the least normal. She'd never seen so much glass and silverware in her life, and it took all her courage to stay dignified in front of the servants. Now, as the butler moved away with the dinner plates, she grimaced. 'I can't go anywhere?'

'You couldn't afford to go anywhere before this anyway.' Alastair smiled across the table at her, his gentleness robbing his words of offence. 'And at least we don't serve you turnip soup.'

'I know. I'm not complaining.' Her sense of humour reasserted itself. But she wished he wouldn't smile like that. It put her right off what she was thinking.

What was it? Oh, right. Not complaining...

'Or at least, not very much,' she added, hauling herself back to the matter in hand. 'I just need to remember not to take my wheelbarrow close to the boundary while I'm working. And I dread long-distance lenses.'

'They haven't placed you as one of the stone-walling team,' Alastair told her. 'Heaven forbid that they do. You're sure the team will stay silent? And the Berics?'

'I'd imagine your money will ensure that,' she said dryly. 'Talk about buying silence. So you're right. As long as I stay here I'm fine.'

'But...' Alastair was thinking this through '...there is one problem. You'll need to take a trip to the city.'

'Why?'

'You need clothes.'

She bristled. 'What's wrong with my clothes?'

He hesitated, and then he smiled again, seeking to lessen offence. 'Your dress...' He motioned to her sundress. 'I know I'm not supposed to notice, but it's the third night in a row that you've worn it.'

Her bristle turned into a glower. 'So? I *like* my dress.'

He raised his eyebrows. 'And you have a wardrobe of different evening-wear?'

'I don't need—'

'A stone-waller may not need, but my intended bride does,' he told her. 'Friday is official announcement time, and you should look great.'

'She looks great now.' Marguerite's warmth and approval were the one constant in this arrangement that was making Penny-Rose feel OK with what was happening, and it came to the fore now. 'The media will love her.'

'Rose was photographed leaving Lilie's in that dress,' Alastair said stubbornly. 'She needs another.'

Marguerite was like a defensive mother hen. 'I'm sure she has another.' And then she frowned at her son. 'Why do you call her Rose? Her name is Penny-Rose.'

'Penny-Rose is hardly a name for a princess. Rose is much more dignified.'

Much more *not me*, Penny-Rose thought. Still, this marriage was all about keeping their distance. If that was the way he wanted it...

It seemed he did.

'Do you have anything else to wear?' he asked, deflecting his mother's query nicely.

'Um...' Penny-Rose turned pink. 'Actually I don't.'

'Oh, my dear...' Marguerite sounded horrified.

'Don't let it bother you,' she said hastily. 'I don't understand what women see in choice. It makes dressing a whole lot more complicated.'

'But it also makes it more fun.' Marguerite had swung to her son's point of view in a moment. 'Now, where will you go to shop? You can't go anywhere in this principality. You'll be mobbed before you reach the first boutique. There's nothing for it. Alastair, you'll have to take her to Paris. You need a few days on the rue du Faubourg Saint Honoré...'

'Hey...' The idea startled him. 'I don't have time to go to Paris. It's not me who needs clothes.'

'She can't shop here.'

'No, but—'

'But Paris it must be. Are you saying that you won't take her?' his mother demanded, and fixed him with a look.

'I could have Belle take her...'

There was a collective intake of breath. And then Alastair had the grace to grimace. 'OK.

Bad idea. Belle's well known and there are media problems everywhere.' He sighed and appealed again to his mother. 'But you're the obvious one to go.'

'No, dear.' His mother shook her head. 'The press has seen you once together. The more romance we can imbue this with, the better. I'm not saying I hope the photographers find you—you need a couple of days' grace—but if they do eventually track you down, it'd be so romantic to have you photographed strolling down Paris streets, hand in hand.'

'Hey, I don't intend holding anyone's hand,' Penny-Rose retorted, and Marguerite sighed again.

'You two aren't very good at this romance business, are you?'

'We're fine,' Alastair said.

'Right. Good. So hold hands.'

'Mother…'

'You need to get used to it.' His mother looked from Penny-Rose to Alastair and back again. 'In six weeks someone's going to say, "You may kiss the bride." If that means one chaste kiss on the forehead, the lawyers will label this marriage a sham and the castle—and the estate—will be lost. To us and to the villagers.'

'They can't—'

'This marriage has to appear real,' Marguerite said with asperity. 'Alastair, stop treating the girl as if she'll bite. Penny-Rose, stop treating the man as if he's your boss. Get friendly.'

'Yes, ma'am,' Penny-Rose said, and she managed a smile. 'I'll do what I can.'

'Alastair, take the girl to Paris. And start calling her Penny-Rose.'

'Um…'

'Don't ''um'' me,' his mother snapped. 'Get a handle on this. You never know, you could just enjoy yourselves.'

'Rose could enjoy shopping on her own.'

'Call her Penny-Rose.'

'It's not a princess's name.'

'And she'll only be a princess? Not a friend?'

'We need to keep things formal.'

'Fine,' his mother said, exasperated. 'Just take what's-her-name to Paris.'

His exasperation equalled his mother's.

'What's-her-name can go alone.'

'Excuse me,' Penny-Rose said, grinning slightly at their matching belligerent expressions. They really were very alike. 'But I…I suspect I might need some help. I don't exactly have much experience in shopping.'

They stopped glaring at each other and turned their stunned attention to her.

'No experience in shopping.' Marguerite gasped. 'Oh, my dear...' She sounded as if she'd just heard Penny-Rose had been deprived of something of major importance. Like a leg.

'So where did you find the dress you're wearing?' Alastair demanded in disbelief. All women shopped!

'Actually, I made it myself. I sew all my own clothes.'

That stunned them even more. Alastair stared at her as if she'd announced that she'd come from another planet.

'You're kidding.' Sewing your own clothes... He'd hardly heard of such a thing.

'I'm not kidding.' She met his look head on, defiant. 'I don't just stone-wall. I have other skills, too.' She grinned. 'I can also whistle loud enough to call the kids home from a mile away. Want to hear?' And she put two fingers to her mouth and prepared to whistle.

'No!' Marguerite and Alastair spoke as one, and she chuckled and desisted, but Alastair was still looking at her dress in awe.

'But...' His critical eyes appraised her workmanship and found no fault at all. 'It's lovely.'

She twinkled. 'Thank you.'

He was still having trouble believing her. 'And…your overalls?'

'I made them, too.'

'You really have never shopped for clothes?'

'Sometimes at welfare places,' she said diffidently. 'But not…not at real clothes shops.'

'Oh, Alastair!' Marguerite's eyes were shining. 'What fun. To introduce your bride to shopping!'

'To introduce your future daughter-in-law to shopping,' he retorted, but despite himself his imagination was caught. 'I don't suppose…' His thoughts were heading off at all sorts of wondrous tangents. A woman who'd never shopped…it was almost unbelievable. 'Things like lacy negligees and so on…' he said slowly. 'I can hardly help her there.'

'Of course you can,' his mother said soundly. 'Now…you're to leave tomorrow morning. You're to stay at the Hotel Carlon, which Belle tells me is the most splendid hotel in Paris. You're to spend a fortune and you're to have a very good time. That's an order. Any questions?'

'No, ma'am,' Penny-Rose said faintly. 'Except…' She blinked. 'There's Bert. I need to ask Bert for a couple of days off.'

'Bert and I have an arrangement,' Alastair told her. 'He's a very understanding boss—and employee.'

That didn't please her. 'You mean you'll just bribe him to keep me on the team with no questions asked.'

'I need do no such thing. He's not about to sack you.'

'He mustn't. If I lose my spot on the team…'

'Because you're out buying frilly knickers…'

'If you so much as tell him that…' She was aghast.

'I won't.' Alastair smiled at her.

Drat! His smile was really starting to get to her. For heaven's sake—she'd been living in Alastair's home for only two days. She had over a year of this mock marriage to go, but there was something very strange going on already. Every time the man smiled at her, something in the deeper recesses of her middle did some sort of stupid lurch…

It was just that he was so darned attractive, she thought wildly, and the number of deeply attractive men she'd spent any time with in her life numbered approximately zero.

Or maybe it was just that she hadn't had time to notice, she decided, forcing herself to be practical. Maybe there were plenty of gorgeous guys out there, and after this wedding farce was over—after her twelve-month marriage—maybe she could see for herself...

With her frilly knickers!

The thought made her grin, and Alastair saw it and smiled back.

'What?'

'Sorry?'

'What are you laughing at?'

'The thought of me in frilly knickers underneath my homemade overalls,' she confessed. 'Some things are too ridiculous for words.'

'But you'll come shopping with me?'

'Do I have a choice?'

'No.'

She spread her hands. 'OK. One shopping hit. But it'll have to be just the one. Let's get it all over in one shot. Can we buy a wedding dress while we're at it?'

'I have an idea about that.' Marguerite had been watching the interplay, a small, self-satisfied smile playing on her lips. Who knew what was behind that smile? 'I thought...' She hesitated. 'My dear, if you don't mind, I thought you could wear my wedding dress.' She flickered a questioning look at her son. 'You've always loved the photographs of your father and I being married. The dress I wore belonged to your grandmother before me, and it's lovely. If Penny-Rose agrees, it'd be wonderful for you to have your bride wear it.'

'But won't Belle...?' Penny-Rose started, but was silenced by the sudden frown snapping down on her future mother-in-law's face.

'Belle would die rather than wear an old dress of mine.'

Belle would. The thought of the svelte Belle wearing a traditional, pre-loved wedding gown seemed almost ridiculous.

'I... It seems very personal,' Penny-Rose said, looking sideways at Alastair to see how he was taking it. 'I mean, it *is* a wedding of convenience. It *is* only for a year.'

But, somewhat to her surprise, Alastair liked the idea. 'I bet it'd look gorgeous on you. And it's very economical.' He smiled. 'That should appeal to your parsimonious streak!'

'If it's your money, I don't mind spending it,' she replied, and got a bark of laughter in response.

'That's very generous.'

'I can be,' she agreed blandly, and just for a moment they were grinning at each other like fools.

Or like...friends?

Or something more.

Which was crazy. But the moment stretched on, for far too long...

It was Alastair who came back to earth first. Penny-Rose's insides were still doing some type of aerobic act she couldn't define. 'You'll wear my mother's dress?' he asked, and if his voice was a trace unsteady it was only Marguerite who noticed. Penny-Rose's thoughts were way too unsteady all on their own.

'Penny-Rose needs to see it first,' Marguerite decreed, smiling complacently at them both. Things were going very well here. Very well indeed! 'She's only wearing it if she loves it. But meanwhile... Eat your supper, turn in for an early night and then head off to Paris in the morning.'

'For knicker shopping,' Alastair agreed, a wicked gleam lurking deep in those dangerous eyes.

'In your dreams, Alastair de Castaliae,' Penny-Rose muttered. 'You buy me frilly knickers? Over my dead body.' She hesitated. 'And maybe it's just as well if we buy me a wedding dress. I'm really not comfortable wearing your mother's.'

'Why not?'

'Because it's real,' she said frankly. Her insides had somehow settled, but with that crazy lurching had come a realisation. Alastair was holding her at arm's length. She needed to do the same. 'Some day you might meet someone even more special than Belle.'

'That's silly.'

'No, it's not.' She turned to Marguerite. 'You must understand. Wearing your wedding dress makes the whole thing personal—and this wedding has to be impersonal or it can't work.'

'I'd like you to wear it,' Marguerite told her, and with a shock Penny-Rose realised what she was saying.

And she knew she was right in her decision.

'I can't,' she told her. 'It's for Alastair's true wife to wear.'

'I don't understand.' Alastair was looking from one to the other. 'You will be my true wife.'

'As I said,' Penny-Rose retorted. 'In your dreams, Alastair de Castaliae. In your dreams.'

The next day was a dream all by itself.

First there was the journey to Paris.

Penny-Rose and her co-workers had taken the train through France when she'd started working in Alastair's tiny border principality, and she'd expected that she and Alastair would take the same train back to Paris. Or they'd drive. Either way, it was a full day's journey.

But they did neither. After an early breakfast, Alastair ushered her into his Ferrari. Ten minutes later they were boarding a private jet, and thirty minutes after that they were at Charles de Gaulle airport.

There was a limousine waiting. Awed into silence, Penny-Rose was ushered into the car like royalty, and she sank back onto leather cushions and thought that was exactly what she was! Royalty.

Sort of.

Or she would be in a matter of weeks, after this fairy-tale wedding had taken place.

And then they reached their hotel. Alastair left her at her suite door and she had to pinch herself to ensure she really was awake.

Her suite was twice as big as the house she'd been raised in. Heck, the bed was almost as big as the house she'd been raised in! There was more gold and silk and brocade than she'd ever seen in her life.

It was great. Great! So why wasn't she bouncing in pleasure?

It was simply too big and too opulent and too damned lonely. Australia and her family seemed suddenly very far away, and she felt herself blinking back a tear.

She wandered around the suite, touching everything, hardly daring to breathe, and when a knock sounded at the door she jumped a foot.

It was Alastair. Of course. She'd been so stunned she'd hardly noticed him leaving to be shown to his own rooms. But all of a sudden she was desperately glad he was back.

This felt over-the-top opulent, and she was way out of her depth.

'This…this is quite some hotel,' she made herself say, and he nodded and watched her face.

'It is. Do you like it?'

She took a deep breath and looked around. And looked around again.

'It lacks something,' she said finally. 'Or some things. It needs half-a-dozen kids, a few cats and dogs, pizza boxes on the floor, a couple of inner tubes and some rubber duckies for the bath, something noisy on television…and maybe then I'd like it. A little bit.'

'You don't like it.'

'Um, no,' she confessed. 'It's like a palace.' She wrinkled her nose. 'You may be used to sleeping in palaces—'

'Hey, I've only just inherited the title.'

'You chose this place.'

'I didn't,' he admitted. 'I've never been in this hotel. But Belle says it's the best and my mother said I should bring you to the best.'

'And you always do what Belle and your mother say. I see.' She chewed her bottom lip. 'My bath,' she said at last, 'is in the shape of a heart. It's a spa with padded seats. Built for two. The bathroom looks as if it's been designed for Cleopatra.'

'Mmm.'

'You have the same?'

He nodded, unsure where the conversation was leading. 'I have the same.'

'So we have a heart-shaped spa each,' she said. 'That's cosy. Two spas built for two. One in each room.'

'You're telling me it's over the top?' he ventured, his lips twitching, and she tilted her chin and nodded.

'Just a bit. Maybe.'

'We could always share.'

'Oh, right.' She gave him an old-fashioned look. 'And then your requirement that I be a virtuous bride goes right out the window.'

'There is that.'

Alastair's smile faded as he assessed his future wife. Dressed casually in tailored trousers and a linen open-necked shirt, Alastair himself looked supremely at ease in these luxurious surroundings. His future bride, however, looked far from comfortable.

It was her hands, he thought. Always his eyes fell to her hands. Her sundress was lovely, she looked lovely, but her hands were the true Rose. Or Penny-Rose. They made him feel wrong—as if he was pushing her into something she wasn't meant to be.

He was suddenly, irresistibly reminded of a television show he'd once seen, where a much-decorated war veteran had been brought in for 'show and tell'. The man's deeds had been awesome, but the television show had been superficial. It had glamorised and in the process somehow belittled both the man and his actions.

He'd been uncomfortable, watching.

He was uncomfortable now.

'Do you really not like it?'

'It's the gilt and the brocade,' she explained. 'And...'

'And what?'

'The mirrors. Wherever I go I see me.'

'I can think of worse things to look at.'

'Yeah, right, when you have Belle to compare me to. I don't think.' She took a deep breath. 'OK. I'll get over it. But I would prefer something a bit simpler.'

'The Hotel Carlon doesn't do simple.'

'Then I'm stuck with it.' She looked down at her sundress and wrinkled her nose. 'But I believe you now when you say I need clothes, especially if I'm to spend any more time in front of these damned mirrors. Fine. Let's get out of here and go shopping.'

'You're seriously not looking forward to this?'

'I'm seriously not looking forward to this.' She grimaced and made a confession. 'I don't exactly know how it's done.'

'What, shopping?'

'Shopping.'

'It's easy,' he told her, suppressing a smile. 'You stand in a shop, you show them your credit card and you watch what happens.' He held out his hand. 'Come and see.'

She stared down at his hand for a long moment. His fingers were tanned and strong and inviting. The gesture to take her hand in his was a casual one, no more.

But what had Marguerite said? *It'd be so romantic to have you...strolling down Paris streets, hand in hand.*

Yeah, great.

But the hand was still proffered, and a deal was a deal. What was the man offering? A million pounds. Whew!

It was the stuff of dreams, and if she was to engage in dreams she might as well go the whole distance.

So she smiled up at her intended husband with a confidence she was far from feeling, she put her hand in his and she let herself be led out onto the streets of Paris.

To shop!

It wasn't an introduction into shopping that Alastair gave her. It was a crash course master's degree and then some. They shopped and shopped and shopped, and when Penny-Rose decided there couldn't be an item of clothing left in Paris that she hadn't tried on, Alastair turned to accessories and shopped some more.

They paused only for meals. He took her to quiet little restaurants where he wasn't likely to be known. They ate wonderful food, but Penny-Rose slipped into a quietness which even Alastair knew was out of character. On their second day he collected her from her room to find she had dark shadows under her eyes, and when questioned she admitted she hadn't slept.

'It's the bed,' she told him. 'It's too big and too cold and too...'

'Too?'

'Lonely.' There. She'd said it. She looked at him, expecting to see laughter, but instead she saw concern.

'Five-star hotels by yourself are a bit echoing,' he agreed. 'My suite's just as barren. But I don't think sharing's an option, do you?'

'No!'

'Then we just get on with it. One more night and then home tomorrow...'

'Home to your castle!'

He thought of the sumptuous guest room in the castle and frowned. 'Do you find that just as lonely?'

'I'm not homesick,' she said, seeing what he was thinking. 'I'm never homesick.'

'No?'

'No,' she lied. 'I'm enjoying myself. These clothes are...fabulous.'

'We have bought some lovely things,' he said gravely. 'And there's more to come.'

Her determined cheerfulness faltered. 'I... Yes.'

'You're not enjoying the shopping either?'

'I feel like a kept woman,' she blurted out. 'It's awful. I don't know that I'm going to be able to stand it for a year.'

'Being a princess?'

'Being a princess.'

He surveyed her face with caution. If he wasn't careful he could blow it, and he knew it.

Most women would jump at the chance she was being offered, he thought, but he knew enough of her now to know that most women didn't include Rose.

'You can back out,' he told her.

'And then what?'

'And then I'd lose my estate and Michael wouldn't go to university.'

'See? We're up against a brick wall—both of us.'

'It's a comfortably padded brick wall,' he said lightly, and she flushed and bit her lip.

'I know. I'm being stupid.'

'It's harder for you than for me,' he acknowledged. 'I'm not being hauled out of my comfort zone.'

Penny-Rose thought that through and found flaws. 'It's not very comfortable, living on turnip soup,' she said, and he smiled. She had courage.

And the only way through this was through it.

'Breakfast?' He proffered his arm.

'Oh, yup, why not? A smorgasbord of two hundred different dishes...'

'Don't tell me you'd prefer a baguette.'

'Well, actually...'

'Actually, yes?'

And there was only one answer to that. The choice in the hotel's lavish restaurant simply overwhelmed her. 'Yes.'

He looked her up and down, and then he sighed. 'Come on,' he said in exasperation. 'Breakfast here is the most magnificent that Paris has to offer, but don't mind that. Let's turn our backs on the Carlon's stupendous breakfast and go find ourselves a baguette.'

'Alastair...'

But he was brooking no argument. 'I can slum it with the best of them,' he told her. His arm linked with hers and held. 'Just watch me.'

CHAPTER FIVE

SO INSTEAD of eating the hotel's sumptuous breakfast they found a patisserie and Alastair proceeded to show Penny-Rose that he had absolutely no idea what slumming meant. As a peasant, he failed miserably. Penny-Rose's simple baguette was simply not enough, not faced with the choice of Paris's magnificent pastries.

So while she watched in open-mouthed amazement, he proceeded to buy one of everything he could see. A baguette, croissants and mouth-watering pastries filled with fruit, something chocolate that Penny-Rose, with her limited French, decided was called Death by Explosion, and more...

Then there was coffee in huge take-away mugs, the smell of which made her mouth water.

They emerged finally from their patisserie to find piles of grapes and mandarins on a next-door stall. Ignoring her protests—'You've dragged me away from the Hotel Carlon's breakfast, woman—you can let me buy what I want'—he loaded them with so much breakfast they were having trouble carrying it. And Penny-Rose was caught between laughter and exasperation.

She was given time for neither. 'Now to the Bois de Boulogne,' Alastair decreed. 'It's the closest.'

It was also the loveliest.

The sun was already warm with the promise of a magnificent day to come. The park was filled with mothers and pushchairs, elderly couples sitting soaking up the sun, and small children playing tag or racing with balloons...

In true royal fashion Alastair found a tree and claimed it as their own. He signalled to someone in the distance, and before she knew it there were two deckchairs set up for their comfort.

'Now...' Alastair surveyed his scene with satisfaction. 'Breakfast as Parisians do it.'

'Oh, right. Parisian princes, would that be?'

'You don't like this either?' His face fell ludicrously and it was all Penny-Rose could do not to laugh.

But he was watching her with such an expression of anxiety on his face—and the sun was warm on hers—and it was Paris in the springtime and the coffee smelled tantalising and the pastries were exquisite...

'I'd have to be a mindless idiot not to enjoy this,' she said softly, smiling up at him. 'No, Alastair, I don't like this. I love it!'

After that the shopping was better, though Penny-Rose still found it uncomfortable. She was now wearing some of the clothes she'd purchased the day before. That made her feel less conspicuous in these over-the-top salons, but every time she dressed at the end of each fitting she couldn't help thinking, These aren't my clothes.

These aren't me.

She was buying clothes for a princess, she thought. Not for Penny-Rose O'Shea. Or two-bob Rose. Or whoever she was. She was beginning not to know any more.

Once he'd made the decision to accompany her, Alastair took his duties seriously. He insisted on seeing her as she emerged in each outfit, and his smiles of approval disturbed her still more. She was turning into what he wanted, she thought.

She was becoming no longer herself. She was becoming Alastair's wife-for-a-year, and the prospect was more and more disturbing.

But finally Alastair was satisfied. Almost. At four o'clock he announced her major wardrobe complete, and he escorted her to a tiny shop off the main boulevard.

The shop needed some explaining, and he did it fast. 'Before you get the wrong idea, my mother told me to bring you here,' he told her hastily. At the look on her face, his dark eyes glinted with laughter. 'This,' he said with an evil grin, 'may well be the best part of the whole shopping experience. It's knicker time.'

And as Penny-Rose gazed into the window she could only gasp.

These weren't just knickers. They were flights of fancy. Here were silken wisps of elegance that had nothing at all in common with the sturdy knickers she was wearing—except maybe two holes for legs.

'I can't buy these!'

Alastair's grin faded. 'You can.' He took her hand, imbuing her with the gravity of the occasion. Only his still-lurking glimmer belied his serious tone. 'And you must. The servants will be doing your washing, and they'll expect quality.' His grin returned in full and she stared at him in confusion. The rat—he was enjoying this! 'Remember,' he told her, 'this marriage has to appear real.'

Somehow she found her voice. 'Your wife would wear things like these?'

He nodded, with no hesitation at all. 'Of course she would.' He motioned to a flagrantly indecent set of bra and panties on a flagrantly indecent model, and his laughter became more pronounced. 'My wife would especially wear those.'

'Oh, yeah, I can see Belle in those!'

His smile faded again, but this time the fading was for real. He hadn't been thinking of Belle, she realised as she watched his face. The rat had actually been thinking of her!

This was crazy. The whole situation was absurd!

'So I'm buying these to keep up appearances with the laundress?' she asked carefully.

'That's right.'

'Does the laundress have any colour preference?'

He pointed to the bra and pantie set—bright crimson. 'I bet bright crimson would work a treat.'

'On the laundress.' She glowered.

He assumed an air of injured innocence. 'Who else could I be thinking of?'

'Right.' Her glower intensified. 'Well, if this is just between me and the laundress, you can take yourself off while I make my purchases.'

'Hey…'

'This is between me and the laundress and the shop assistant,' she said firmly. 'Back in your box, mister.'

'That's no way to talk to a prince.'

'A princess can talk any way she wants. And you want a virtuous bride. Virtuous brides wouldn't be seen dead in a shop like this, especially with their prince—and especially before they're married.'

He thought that one through and didn't like it. 'That's not playing fair.'

'Who's playing?'

Their eyes locked.

And suddenly the question was very, very real.

Who was playing? Who could tell?

The scary part was that somewhere in that over-the-top place Penny-Rose finally started to enjoy herself. With Alastair firmly left outside, she let the sales assistant have her head and she tried on set after set of the most gorgeous lingerie she'd ever seen in her life.

And standing in front of the three-way mirror she started to get an inkling of how Cinderella must have felt.

'It's an out-of-body experience,' she told herself, looking at her trim body clothed only in a

wisp of lace that could well have been cut—
with cloth left over—from a very small handkerchief. She grinned. 'Or an only-just-in-body
experience. I guess when this is all done I can
donate these to charity.'

Charity would have a fit, she decided, and it
was with a chuckle and arms full of packages
that she emerged to the street to find her waiting prince.

But her prince wasn't where she'd left him.
She searched the street, and found...

A dog. A pup...

The pup was some sort of terrier, knee high,
wire-haired and fawn and white. Or he might
once have been fawn and white. Now his fur
was matted and filthy, and a deep, jagged
wound stretched along most of his side. One
leg was carried high, his shaggy ears drooped
and his eyes were dull with misery.

It was the end of a Paris business day. The
boulevard was crowded, with legs going everywhere. Even though Paris was a city of dog
lovers, in this crowd one small dog didn't stand
a chance of being noticed. Except by Penny-
Rose, who was feeling bereft herself and was
searching for Alastair.

She saw the dog first. As she emerged from
the shop and saw him, the small creature was

pushed too close to the road, and she realised how he'd got that wound. He was headed that way again.

'No!' With a cry of dismay she dropped her parcels and darted forward. She was too late to stop the dog being pushed onto the road, but that didn't stop her from diving after him. There was a screech of brakes, and the next moment she was crouched in the gutter, her arms were full of dog and her eyes were reflecting his pain.

'Oh, no...'

'Rose!'

Alastair had been waiting with the patience of a saint—sort of. He'd been across the road, window-shopping and desperately trying not to think of what his intended wife was doing. He hadn't succeeded. For some reason, all he could think of was his bride wearing that lingerie...

So he hadn't noticed the dog through the mass of legs across the street, and the first thing he saw was Rose diving head first into the crazy Parisian traffic.

Hell! What on earth...? His heart hit his mouth. He lunged across the road, ignoring braking cars. Reaching the gutter where she knelt, he looked down in consternation.

What was wrong? Had she been hit?

'Are you…' His voice was a cracked whisper as he stooped urgently toward her. 'Rose, are you OK?'

'Yes.' She didn't even look up.

His breath came out in a long rush. Dear God…

'What…what on earth are you doing?'

'It's a dog,' she said, as if he were stupid. But he wasn't. After that heart-stopping moment when he thought she'd been hit, his brain was starting to function again. A taxi veered toward them, and before she knew what he was about, she was bodily lifted and carried back toward the shops.

'You'll get yourself killed!' Alastair had been badly shaken and it showed. 'Are you crazy?'

But Penny-Rose wasn't noticing, not even when he carried her across the pavement to the safety of the shop doorway. She had eyes only for the dog she carried. Alastair set her down, and her fingers kept probing, parting matted fur so she could see the damage.

What was wrong with him?

The dog lay limp and unresisting in her arms, past caring. Alastair knelt beside her, and watched woman and dog together. He felt as if all the breath had been knocked out of him.

'Let me see.'

'He's...he's injured.' She opened her arms so Alastair could see the state of her small burden, and it was all Alastair could do not to wince at the sight.

'Hell!'

Penny-Rose wasn't listening. Pedestrians were having to detour around her, but she didn't notice. She sat with her back against the door of the lingerie shop, and her whole attention was on one small dog.

'It's OK,' she comforted him. 'It's OK, little one. You're fine now.'

Only he wasn't fine. He needed a vet.

'Alastair...'

He was way in front. 'Paris is a dog-loving city,' he said, kneeling beside her. He knew without being asked that she'd never abandon this mutt—and in truth he felt the same himself. The dog was gazing at him now, and there was something about those huge brown, pain-filled eyes... 'There are organisations who take in strays, and there are veterinary surgeons everywhere. I'll call a taxi and we'll take him to the closest.'

She breathed a long sigh. She wasn't sure what she'd expected—she knew this man so little—but all she knew now was that he hadn't reacted like her father.

Her father would have taken one look at the dog—and one look at his daughter's concerned face—and fetched his gun.

But Alastair was different! His first thought hadn't been how best to be rid of the problem and how to hurt her in the process, but how best they could help the dog.

He was some man, she thought dazedly.

He was some prince!

But she needed to concentrate on the dog. She turned back to her pup, cradling him close to give him some body warmth. 'He's only a baby.' The pup was still at the gangly half-grown stage, when dogs were most at risk, out-growing their cuteness and risking abandonment in the process. 'And he's shaking all over.'

'I'd imagine he must be. He looks as if he's been hit by a car.'

'And he's starving. His ribs... Oh, pup...'

'Come on.' Alastair made a decision and glanced round the street with a rueful smile. 'You can't stay here.'

For the first time she seemed to take in her surroundings. They were hardly dignified. She was sitting in the dust with her stockinged legs

out in front of her. She'd lost a shoe. The pup
was curled into her lap. Her pale lemon suit was
filthy, there was blood on her skirt and she must
look...

She didn't get any further. A flashbulb went
off not four feet from her face.

She looked up blindly and the flash went
again.

The cameraman had been in a nearby café
and had been attracted by the screech of brakes.
This had the makings of a great photo oppor-
tunity, he'd thought as he'd watched what had
unfolded—a beautiful woman crouched on the
pavement among scattered shopping, her arms
full of bloodied dog.

So, while the rest of Paris had gone about its
business, he'd hauled his camera out of his bag
and headed over to take a few snaps.

Penny-Rose looked up, her face uncompre-
hending. What...?

'Let her be,' Alastair growled, and the man's
attention turned to him. His eyes widened in
shock.

Alastair de Castaliae!

Alastair wasn't as well known in Paris as he
was in his own country but this cameraman was
on the fringe of the paparazzi. He knew his ce-
lebrities! In one instant his face changed. He

saw a fortune dangling before his eyes, and his camera turned onto automatic.

In the next thirty seconds he'd taken maybe a dozen shots—of the couple crouched on the pavement, of the girl trying to protect her dog from the flash of the camera, and Alastair using his body to shield her.

Which left Alastair in a dilemma. Stopping the camera was impossible. Short of doing the man harm, he had to be allowed to take what he wanted.

He had a choice. He could treat the cameraman as the enemy—which would get them nowhere—or he could treat him as an accomplice, which might achieve more.

'OK, we're sprung.' Alastair sighed, letting his shielding hand drop. 'Any chance of doing a deal?'

'What sort of deal?' The man was still behind his camera, still clicking, but his mind was in overdrive. There'd be at least three major newspapers who'd bid for these pictures, and that was just in France. In Alastair's principality there'd be more, and then there were the women's magazines...

Alastair could see the way his mind was working. And his thoughts had to move even faster.

'We're making an announcement on Friday,' Alastair told him. 'Back home. Would you like to be around when we do?'

The man's eyes practically started from his head. He was only just getting a toehold in this industry, and this could be the break he'd been looking for.

'Sure.' His camera was lowered as he stared in disbelief. 'Yeah, great.'

'Then give us a day before you publish these pictures,' Alastair said. 'One more day of peace.'

'You're marrying the girl?' The man looked closely at Penny-Rose and tried for the jackpot. 'Will you tell me your name?'

'As I said, we're making an announcement on Friday.' Alastair refused to be drawn further, and Penny-Rose took her cue from him.

What else could it be but an announcement of a marriage? The cameraman knew the conditions of the old prince's will. All the paparazzi did. It was their business to know.

'And you're taking a last fling in Paris before the world catches up with you?' The photographer was a romantic at heart, and he could see the headlines over his pictures. He took an uneasy glance along the street. The last thing he wanted now was someone else with a camera. He wanted a scoop!

And Alastair was as eager to get off the street as the cameraman now was to have them leave. He hauled out a business card and scribbled something on the back. 'Here. Ring this number, ask to speak to Dominic and he'll organise you a free return flight.'

'You're kidding!'

'I'd never kid about something like this.'

The man stared down at the card and his face twisted. And he decided on a bit of honesty himself. 'You know, this could be just what I need…'

'I know. But *we* need another day by ourselves.'

The man hesitated. 'I won't be scooped?'

'Not if you keep your mouth shut for twenty-four hours.'

'I can do that.' The photographer grinned, making up his mind. 'One more day with your lady, your dog and your…' His grin broadened. 'Your lingerie.'

With a gasp, Penny-Rose realised what had happened. She'd thrown aside her bags as she'd dived for the dog. She was now sitting among a pile of…

Oh, good grief!

'Can you edit those out?' Alastair demanded, glancing around at the wisps of silk. He fished in his wallet. 'I'll make it worthwhile.'

'Nothing would make editing this out worthwhile,' the man said bluntly. Then, as Alastair signalled for a taxi, he threw in a last question. 'The dog—I assume it's a stray?'

'I imagine he is,' Penny-Rose said shortly.

'Are you keeping it?'

A taxi drew to a halt. Alastair helped Penny-Rose to her feet and thankfully she tumbled into the car, still clutching her pup.

'Just tell me,' the photographer said, this time more urgently. *'Are you keeping the dog?'*

Alastair was gathering knickers and bras and shopping bags together. They needed to get out of there, fast!

'Are you keeping it?' the photographer demanded a third time, and Alastair turned to Rose.

Her face was white and strained. She'd had enough, he knew. These days in unfamiliar territory had taken their toll.

She was so far from home, he thought as he watched her hug the pup. She'd come close to being killed, she was badly shocked, and now... Suddenly he realised he'd never seen anyone look so alone.

She wasn't alone. She was with him. He needed her—and if he wasn't careful he'd lose himself a wife!

Were they keeping the dog? She was holding on as if she needed the pathetic little creature more than the pup needed her.

'Yes,' Alastair said strongly, and with the same flash of insight that had seen her homesickness, he knew this was the only sensible thing to do. 'Of course we're keeping the dog. Why not?'

The cab driver took them to the nearest veterinarian.

'Not to the animal shelter?' Penny-Rose asked, and Alastair shook his head. For some reason he was unsure what to say—they were both in unfamiliar territory.

So they stayed silent while the vet clucked over the little dog, cleaned and stitched the gash on his side, examined his leg and told them the pup was starving but the leg itself was just badly bruised.

'Take him home and give him a light meal— not too much as his stomach won't be accustomed to big feeds. Look after him well, Madame.'

The vet smiled, speaking in halting English. Normally this man didn't deign to use English—it was his opinion that foreigners should speak French in France—but there was something about Penny-Rose that made a man want to help all he could. Her halting thanks in French had made him smile. 'Though I have no need to tell you to take care of him,' he said gently. 'I believe you are doing so already.'

Unlike the photographer, he didn't ask if she intended keeping him. That was assumed.

But she'd been thinking, and there were problems.

'I don't think I *can* take him,' she faltered as they emerged again to the streets of Paris. She looked up and found Alastair's eyes gravely watchful. 'At the end of the year I need to go home. The quarantine between here and Australia takes months.'

'What's a few months between friends?' Alastair smiled. OK, if he was getting committed, he might as well get really committed. To a dog, mind, he told himself hastily. Just to a dog! 'If there are problems, I'll look after him when you go.' He looked down at the disreputable mutt, the pup looked mournfully back and Alastair's grin broadened. OK. Commitment here didn't seem too hard. 'My castle could do with an aristocratic hound as watch dog.'

'Alastair...' Penny-Rose caught her breath at the enormity of his offer. She felt like she'd been handed the crown jewels. 'You're kidding?'

'Would I kid about something that means so much?'

She stared up at him, and something caught in her throat. Penny-Rose had never been handed a gift like this in her life. Gifts weren't something that came in her direction—ever.

With a struggle she kept her voice light, though she felt tears of gratitude welling and it was all she could do to fight them back. 'An...an aristocratic hound,' she managed. 'I don't think so.'

'He'll do.'

She thought about this. 'As I'll do for a wife. Make-believe until the real thing comes along.'

'That's right.' He was looking at her strangely, and her insides were kicking—hard.

Someone had to be practical.

Penny-Rose had to be practical! It was the only way if she wasn't going to sink into the man's chest and sob.

'Well, let's go, then.' She set her chin with resolution. 'Take us home. Your temporary

wife and your aristocratic hound. You're getting yourself quite a collection, Alastair de
Castaliae.'

'I believe I am,' Alastair murmured.

And he didn't look like a man fighting
against the odds one bit.

To her surprise their cab didn't take them back
to Hotel Carlon.

'I've arranged something different,' Alastair
told her as they drove in the opposite direction.
'While you were trying on knickers, I made a
few phone calls and had our bags moved.' He
grinned. 'Maybe it's just as well. Something
tells me Scruffy will be more comfortable
there.'

'Scruffy...' She was confused, but recovering. 'Who are you calling Scruffy?'

'Not you.' Alastair's eyes teased her.
'Though come to think of it...' At the look in
her eyes he held up his hands in mock defence.
'No. The pup. Of course I mean the pup.
Scruffy.'

'His name,' she said with injured dignity, 'is
not Scruffy.'

'Well, what else would you call him?'

Scruffy! Humph. 'His name is Leo.' With her
equilibrium almost restored, with it came de-

cisiveness. She raised her eyebrows with aristocratic hauteur, a princess in the making. 'It means king.'

'A king.' He sounded stunned. 'Like in Leo the lion?' He looked down at the bandaged, bedraggled mutt in her arms, his lips twitched and he nodded. 'Oh, right. I see it.'

'You will.' She smiled. 'Just wait until he recovers.'

'So I have a Leo and a Rose,' he told her, but he was half talking to himself. 'What next?'

What next indeed?

What next was introducing her to their hotel, which was pure pleasure. Penny-Rose walked through unassuming street doors and was stunned into silence, but this time it wasn't grandeur that was taking her breath away. It was loveliness.

The hotel's two floors were sedate and low. Built in pink-washed stone, the buildings circled a cobbled courtyard. French windows opened out to the garden, and her first impression was the fluttering of soft drapes in the evening air.

And that air was gorgeous! The courtyard was a mass of flowers. Wisteria clung to hundred-year-old vines, there were early roses, del-

icate pink tulips, soft blue forget-me-nots...
And more.

The hotel itself looked almost inconspicuous
in the garden setting. Chairs and tables were
scattered under the trees, comfortable and inviting. There was a well-used birdbath, a sculp-
ture of a woman drooping over a fishpond;
there was the gurgle of running water behind...

This was just fabulous, Penny-Rose decided,
and when Alastair showed her to her room—
no porters here—it was even better. Her bedroom was simplicity itself, its major adornment
being the window-framed courtyard. There was
crisp white linen, fluffy white towels, a bath
with no fancy gadgets at all, mounds and
mounds of pillows and...

A dog basket!

She looked an astonished question at
Alastair. How had he managed this?

'I told Madame what our problem was,' he
told her. 'She moves fast. Someone will be here
any minute with minced steak for Leo.'

'Oh, Alastair...' She found herself suddenly
close to tears again. Drat the man. She didn't
give way to emotion—she *never* gave way to
emotion—and here he was unsettling her as no
one else could.

As usual, when things got too much for her she resorted to practical matters. Or tried to. 'Thank you,' she said simply. 'But...' She glanced at her watch. It was well past eight and even her own stomach was rumbling. 'How...how can *we* eat?'

'We're in the middle of the best eating district in Paris. We can eat any time we want.'

She bit her lip. He'd done so much already, and this was hard. 'I mean... I can't leave Leo.'

'Now, how did I know you'd say that?' He smiled down at her, that heart-stopping smile that made her insides do somersaults. 'No problem. While you feed Leo I'll make a foray out into the big, bad world and bring us back food. We can eat in the courtyard.'

'Two picnics in one day!'

He nodded. 'I can handle it. Can you?'

'Yes. Oh, yes.'

She couldn't think of anything more perfect.

CHAPTER SIX

So WHILE Leo, fed and cuddled and exhausted, slept as he'd never slept in his life before, his new owners ate *pâté de fois gras*, then succulent beef, cooked to perfection in a rich Burgundy sauce, with tiny button mushrooms and crusty bread to soak up the juice. Followed by cheeses...

By the time the last of the main meal was gone, Penny-Rose knew she'd been to heaven and back. This was food at its most exquisite served in take-away containers as if it were everyday food.

And there was more! With the air of a magician conjuring up a rabbit or two, Alastair poured a rich, crimson wine that was full of the sunlight of late harvest, and when he produced bite-sized meringues, luscious strawberries and lashings of clotted cream, she could hardly believe her eyes. She'd never eaten like this.

She hadn't known such food existed!

'I can't believe you found all this,' she told him and he looked smug. In truth, he was enjoying himself hugely. He was accustomed to women who treated great food as an everyday event. Rose's delight made him smile.

It also made his chest expand a notch or two. 'I'm a hunter-gatherer from way back,' he said as his smug look intensified. 'There's not a lot me and my trusty club can't do.' He pointed to the remnants of the beef. 'That's Brontosaurus Rex. Or ex-Rex. Whatever.' He pushed his chest out another notch. 'But there's no need to congratulate me. A man does what he must in order to survive.'

'Yeah, right. You survive on this kind of food?'

'I can survive on less,' he told her. 'If I need to. One Rex drumstick instead of two.' His smile faded. 'As I imagine you have in the past.'

Unaware of the way his gaze had just changed, she popped a strawberry into her mouth and sighed in bliss. 'Oh, yes. You know, I may well go home at the end of our twelve-month marriage the size of a house.'

'That's fine by me.' More of Rose? He could handle that.

Her smile disappeared as she thought about it. 'I guess...me getting fat would give you your excuse to divorce me.'

'I doubt anyone would think that was a reasonable excuse,' he said, and suddenly thought, Hell, what excuse was he going to use? Mutual incompatibility?

The more he was getting to know her, the more that reason wouldn't wash.

'It'll have to be homesickness on my part,' she said, watching his face and guessing where his thoughts were headed. 'Or I'll suddenly find out about Belle.'

'And you didn't know about Belle beforehand?'

'I was stupid,' she said cheerfully. 'Thick as a brick. I can be when I want to be. Or even...' her smile deepened '...when I don't want to be.' She decided to confess all. 'You know, the day before we came here, I started adding a fourth layer to my wall without putting in throughstones.'

'Throughstones?' He was lost.

'Stones stretching across the wall to tie the sides,' she said patiently. 'Ask Bert how stupid that is.'

'I...um...I see. An unforgivable sin.'

'You'll think so if your wall falls down in two hundred years,' she retorted, and he smiled.

'I'll be watching for it.'

'And you'll deduct the cost of repair from my wages? That'd be right.'

'Or from your great-great-grandchildren's wages,' he told her. 'Remind me to put something in my will to that effect. My great-great-grandchildren can gather stupidity compensation when it's due.'

'It won't be necessary,' she said with dignity. 'I was only three stones along before I realised. The throughstones are now in place.'

'You relieve my mind enormously.'

'That's the plan.' Her green eyes twinkled and a faintly remembered phrase came wafting thought her consciousness. 'After all, as long as domestic service survives, the convenience of the employer comes first.'

He grinned at that. 'Very good. I like it. And it's not convenient to me if my wall falls down.'

'That's the ticket.' She chuckled. 'Your wife and your dog will have fallen down in their duty, and that would never do.'

It took Alastair a while to answer that. He sat and watched her as she tackled a last strawberry. The day had taken its toll. She looked ruffled and tired, but she'd showered and changed into her own faded jeans and cotton blouse. She looked fresh and clean and lovely—but she was as far from the circle of women he usually moved in as she could be. Her toes were bare, her hair was gently stirring in the warm night air and she wasn't wearing a scrap of make-up.

Domestic servant?

She was Cinderella to a tee, he thought ruefully. But all at once he knew that if the fairy godmother were to arrive with her magic wand, he wouldn't have her wave it.

'I suppose not,' he said at last, and he sounded suddenly bewildered.

But Penny-Rose's own confusion was settling. The last rays of evening sun were lingering over the courtyard, with their echoes of warmth from a perfect spring day. Her little dog lay fast asleep in her room. Soon she'd go up to him, and sleep in her wonderful bed, and wake tomorrow morning to sunshine and...

And to Alastair.

The direction her thoughts were headed suddenly jarred home with a vengeance, and her eyes flew wide with shock.

'What's wrong?' Alastair saw the look.

'I...'

'Rose?'

'Sorry.' She shook her head. 'It's nothing.'

'But something's bothering you.'

'No. It was just something…' She fought for an explanation—any explanation—because the real one surely wouldn't do. 'It was something I forgot to tell Bert, but it'll be OK.'

'You're not still worrying about your wall?' He was gently teasing, but the concern in his voice deepened her sense of shock.

Because she knew now what was happening. There was no question about it. It had never happened in her life before—it was something she'd read about but had never believed was real—but there was now no doubting its reality.

It was happening to her right now.

Help!

'We can go home tomorrow—back to your precious stone-walling,' Alastair was saying, and she had to concentrate fiercely to hear him. 'The only task we have left is to order your wedding dress.'

She thought that through. They'd left her wedding dress to the end of their stay because they knew their chances of making such a purchase without publicity were remote. But now it didn't matter. Tomorrow was Thursday. They'd make their purchase and then they'd fly home to announce their plans.

But Penny-Rose's plans had suddenly changed.

A wedding for a year...

She looked at Alastair and the familiar lurch happened all over again. She knew it now for what it was. It was inescapable, and it had changed things for ever.

This was serious commitment, she thought desperately. This man was *some* prince and he was offering her marriage. It might only be for a year, but she'd still agreed to marry him. What would she say?

'With this ring I thee wed. With my body I thee worship...'

The words of the wedding vow came to her as clearly as a song on the late night air.

'To love and to cherish... From this day forward...'

They'd be making the vows in jest—to last for a year.

But why?

Alastair wasn't in love with Belle. Penny-Rose's thoughts were flying every which way and it was a wonder she wasn't saying things out loud. Confusion was certainly washing over her face. He wasn't in love with anyone, she thought. After the shock of Lissa's death, Alastair had been deeply wary of commitment. He wanted a wife of convenience, and that was all.

So...she was to be his wife of convenience for a year and after that she'd be followed by another convenient bride.

Belle.

It was all wrong, she thought wildly. This man should be loved to distraction. He deserved to be loved to distraction.

As Leo was going to be. As much as she was capable of loving.

Or...as she loved already.

This had never happened to her before, but she knew she was right. Somehow her heart had been handed over, like it or not. Whether or not it was sensible, she was head over heels in love with Alastair de Castaliae, and she didn't know what to do with it.

But she knew now that when she made her wedding vows, she'd be incapable of lying.

'From this day forward...' There'd be a part of her that was desperate for those words to mean exactly what they said. And they meant for ever.

If that was what she wanted...

The old Penny-Rose was surfacing. The Penny-Rose who was prepared to fight and steal and do anything she must to protect her sisters and brother. The Penny-Rose who knew the only way to get what she wanted was to fight with everything she possessed and then more.

Well, maybe she didn't have enough armoury to win this battle, but she knew where she'd start.

'I don't think I will buy a wedding dress,' she told him, fighting to keep her voice casual and watching his face as she did.

He frowned, thrown off balance. 'Why not?' He hesitated, and the forlorn look she'd been wearing came back to him. 'You're not thinking of pulling out, are you?' His voice was anxious. Hell, if she pulled out now... 'You'll still marry me?'

'Now, what have you done in the last couple of hours to make me change my mind?' she teased. 'You've been a model fiancé.'

The lurching in the pit of his stomach settled. A bit. 'Gee, thanks.'

'Think nothing of it.' And then her smile died. 'I've... It's just I've been thinking about your mother's offer.' She bit her lip, hardly daring to go on, but her commitment had already been made, and she had no control over it now. She was suddenly playing for keeps and, whether Alastair knew it or not, his precious independence was in deadly trouble.

But she couldn't tell him that. She had to keep her voice practical and sensible. As all her plans must be.

'I'm tired of spending your money, and I'm tired of shopping,' she declared. 'I've decided I'll wear your grandmother's wedding dress after all.'

'But...' He frowned. 'I thought you objected to the idea. That it's for my true wife to wear.'

'Belle doesn't want to wear it, and you said that's what I'll be,' she told him. 'Your legal wife. For a year.'

And however long I can manage, she told herself silently. From this day forward... For ever if I can manage it.

Penny-Rose lay in bed that night and thought, 'What have I done?'

Beside her, Leo slept the sleep of the dead. Filled with food for maybe the first time in his life, his wounds eased with painkillers and his body snuggled into soft cushions, he lay beside his new mistress and thought he was in doggy heaven.

Her fingers trailed down to touch the pup's wet nose, and she thought she was pretty much in the same place.

But not doggy heaven. Penny-Rose heaven.

'He's given me so much,' she told the sleeping Leo, her conscience giving her a swift kick in the ribs. 'He's handed me a dream for a year. And he's handed me you. It's dreadful of me to go for more.'

But that was just what she was doing. Because somewhere during the last few days, something strange had happened. Her heart had been twisted and turned till she hardly knew herself.

'I've fallen in love,' she whispered. 'So help me, Leo, I've fallen for the man. Now what?'

Fight?

'Just try,' she said to the darkened room. 'Just…take this marriage as it comes but say my vows as if I mean them. And then cross every finger and every toe that I can work a little magic. See if I can change his formal Princess Rose into a Penny-Rose he can love.

'And you'll wear his mother's wedding dress?'

She was questioning her own motives. Leo wuffled in his sleep and Penny-Rose grimaced and buried her nose in the soft pillows.

'It's very wrong.

'But if you don't try…

'If you don't try then Belle will end up with her prince,' she told herself. 'Or with *my* prince.

And he doesn't want her any more than he wants me. It's such a waste!

'So what makes you think you can win his heart?

'Nothing at all.' She was two voices. The voice of reason and the voice of hope. 'Nothing at all,' she repeated into the stillness. 'Oh, but, Leo, I can only try!

'You'll have to do more than try, girl.

'I'll do whatever it takes,' she said, with a resolution she was far from sure of. 'That and a bit more. Heaven help me, I can't do anything else.'

She flicked on her light with sudden determination and crossed to where the day's parcels had been stacked. In a minute she'd discarded her much-patched pyjamas and was standing in front of the mirror.

She was now wearing one of today's purchases—a soft white nightgown of the sheerest silk. It was cut low across her breasts, it was embroidered white on white with tiny rosebuds and she'd never seen anything so exquisite in her life.

'I can't wear this,' she told her reflection. 'I bought this for the laundress.'

Her curls were tumbled to her shoulders, her face was tinged with a faint embarrassed pink and the reflection that looked at her was...

'I'm not wasting this on the laundress,' she addressed the sleeping Leo. She gave her reflection a rueful grimace. 'It makes me look almost lovely.

'Lovelier than Belle?'

She glowered. 'It doesn't matter how lovely Belle is. She doesn't love him.'

And she herself did!

Alastair was sleeping just the other side of the wall. This was a suite, meant for a family. A door connected the rooms. All she had to do was turn the key on her side, and Alastair turn the key on his...

If I was a bit more brazen I'd knock, she thought suddenly, and then she gasped and took a step back as she realised where her thoughts were taking her. 'Penny-Rose O'Shea... You hussy!' she said aloud.

'If that's what it takes,' her reflection answered her.

'Nope.' She slid the nightgown off and reached for her pyjamas. 'I'm not into seduction.

'So what are you into?

'I'm into loving the man to bits,' she responded to herself. 'It's all I have, and if that's not enough…'

The nightie lay on the floor and mocked her.

'We'll see,' she said, and grinned. 'All's fair in love and war. This is a combination of both!'

And in the next room, Alastair lay and stared at the ceiling with a lot more uncertainty. There were things going on in his life that he no longer understood.

It had all seemed so straightforward, he thought grimly. After Lissa's death he'd made the decision to stay uninvolved, and he'd succeeded. His life was what he wanted.

He had a profession he was proud of. He had more than enough money. And he had Belle, available when he needed her, with the thought of a couple of children down the track.

Children…

They'd be quiet little things, he thought, conjuring them from the darkness. Maybe they'd have pigtails and hula hoops. Whatever, they'd be kids for his mother to pamper…

Marguerite deserved grandchildren.

He checked out his vision of his children— but something strange was happening. Instead of faceless prettiness, as there always had been, he now had Penny-Rose's face before him.

Rose, he told himself. It's Rose... Not Penny-Rose. It was stupid, but it was important somehow. He had to keep this formal.

So she was Rose. But why did his kids suddenly have Rose's twinkle, and Rose's cheekiness, and...?

For heaven's sake, no! If they had personality like Penny-Rose—no, *Rose*—then how could he not love them? he thought, and loving anything...

It didn't work. He'd watched his mother break her heart when his father had died, and his own gut had been wrenched enough when Lissa had been killed. Lissa had been such a good friend that the hurt had been dreadful.

So... It was a lesson he'd learned the hard way, but he'd learned it well. You don't give your heart!

He wasn't giving his heart now. This was a marriage of convenience.

What had Rose said? 'The convenience of the employer comes first.'

That was what he was, he thought grimly. An employer. He was paying her to be his wife for a year, and emotional ties didn't come into it.

How could they? She didn't need him long term. That was why he'd chosen her. She was Australian, and she'd be off home as soon as she had her money.

Leaving him with Belle.

Which was the way he wanted it, he told himself hastily. The way it had to be.

The sensible way.

As was Rose's decision to wear his mother's wedding dress. It was economical. Wedding dresses—especially ones suitable for a royal wedding—cost a fortune. She was saving him money with her decision.

Putting the convenience of the employer first!

So why didn't she feel like one of his employees?

'I'm not very good at this Cinderella thing,' he said out loud. 'I'm not comfortable with it. It's the fact that she has nothing and deserves so much that's making this all so damned gut-wrenching.

'That's why you gave her the dog.

'That's right. She has nothing. A dog can't hurt.

'And you're comfortable with her wearing your mother's wedding dress?

'It's sensible.

'Hell!'

He turned over and pummelled his pillows, trying not to envisage Rose in his mother's wedding dress. And then trying not to envisage Rose sleeping just through the wall. Could he hear her? There was a soft murmuring through the door. She was awake. She was probably lonely. All he had to do, he thought, was take his key and—

No!

That was the way of madness. He had to stop Rose from turning into Penny-Rose every time he thought of her.

But she was so close…

How could he block her out? Out of his thoughts? Out of his life?

He'd ring Belle, he decided. She'd talk sense into him. He'd phone her and talk through the Palmerstone job. They'd been working on it together, so she wouldn't think it was strange…

It was one in the morning!

He put the phone down with a reluctant grin. This was *not* a good plan. Belle would think such a phone call was weird. He'd never hear the end of it.

But he had to speak to someone or he'd go nuts.

'What I need,' he told the darkness, 'is another Leo. I wonder whether Rose will let me share...'

His key lay in his hand, and he held it so hard that it hurt.

CHAPTER SEVEN

'JUST leave everything to me.'

Back at the castle, groomed to an inch of her life, Penny-Rose was waiting to become Alastair's official fiancée. They'd called a press conference, the gallery was packed and it was all Penny-Rose could do not to bolt for Australia.

She might have recovered her equilibrium since Paris, she thought desperately. She might have made a few resolutions, but she wasn't a limelight kind of girl.

'This is Belle's forte,' she muttered. 'Can't a substitute wife do as well?'

'You *are* a substitute wife,' Alastair reminded her, and she grimaced.

Oh, great. As if she needed reminding of *that*.

'You don't need to be nervous. Leave the talking to me.'

'I can't do much else with my grasp of French,' she said bitterly. Then she took two deep breaths and got a grip. Cowardice was not what was needed. Resolution was what was needed. From this moment on.

'I do know a phrase that might be useful,' she said thoughtfully. 'How about, *Vous ne me ferez jamais parler*?' She clutched her throat with melodramatic flourish. '*Jamais, jamais, jamais...*'

'*You'll never make me talk*,' Alastair translated faintly. He grinned as the tension eased a bit. '*Never, never, never*. Very useful. Where on earth did you learn that?'

She arched her eyebrows in superior fashion. 'Where else but from my "Use-full Frase For Toorist" book? It's the same place I learned *I am bleeding to death*, *That man has a gun* and *Can you tell me how to reach the border*?' She managed a smirk. 'See? I'm ready for anything.'

Alastair choked on laughter and the tension dissipated even further. But... This was serious. 'As I said, maybe it's best if I do the talking. Most of the press have a solid grasp of English, but—'

'But you don't want me to mess things up by threatening border runs.' Penny-Rose nodded her understanding. 'OK. I know my place. We Cinderella types are designed to sit and simper and look beautiful, and hope like hell the pumpkins stay at bay.'

'Rose…'

She put up her hands. 'I know. I know. I'm being paid heaps, and I'll be good. I promise.' Then she peeped through a crack in the door, trying to see what was waiting for them. 'I wonder if our cameraman from Paris is here? That'll be one friendly face.'

'Yeah, he knows us intimately, right down to the colour of your knickers.' Alastair grimaced.

'He doesn't know the real me wears cotton-tails.'

'Cotton-tails?' Alastair said faintly. 'What are—'

'You don't want to know.' She chuckled. 'If you want to keep your delusion that real women wear black lace thongs, it's fine by me. Oh, he is here. I can see him.'

'He'll be here.' Marguerite was fluttering round the edges, adjusting Alastair's tie and putting one last dab of powder on Rose's nose. 'He'd be mad not to be. A new princess… It's what the press have been waiting for for years.'

'Then let's not keep them waiting.' Alastair's mind was still on the cotton-tail conversation and he was finding it hard to concentrate. But he had to get a grip. Somehow… He swung the door wide. 'But, Rose, for heaven's sake, *leave the talking to me!*'

Only, of course, she couldn't. Because, after the first brief announcement, the press didn't want to hear from Alastair alone. They knew this man. Who they didn't know was the lady he was with, and they were fascinated.

'Tell us about yourself,' one asked in English, and Penny-Rose hesitated, obedient to instruction.

'May I leave that to my—'

'No,' she was told very definitely, and before Alastair could get a word in they'd pushed her further. 'Tell us what you think of our country.'

Well, she'd been obedient for all of a minute. It hadn't worked. So what else was a girl to do but tell the truth?

'It's the most beautiful country I've ever been in,' she said frankly. And then, despite her nervousness, her eyes twinkled. 'Apart from mine.'

'You love Australia?'

'Of course I do!'

'Then what's the attraction here?'

She rolled her eyes at that, and turned toward her intended. She looked Alastair up and down, taking in his immaculate suit and gorgeous tie and the way his eyes creased into laughter lines and…and all of him. Her laughter lines creased into readiness.

'Need you ask?' She chuckled, and the room laughed with her.

They loved her. There were flashbulbs going everywhere and the questioning intensified.

'People are saying this is a marriage of convenience,' she was told. 'What do you say to that?'

Alastair opened his mouth to answer, but his bride-to-be was in her stride and unstoppable.

'They're right, of course.' Her twinkle stayed firmly in place. The only way to meet an accusation of an arranged marriage was partial honesty. 'I imagine you know the terms of my future husband's inheritance? If he doesn't marry then the estate will be dispersed and that'll cause hardship. So…'

Her eyes strayed around the members of the press and it was as if she was speaking to each person in turn. In moments, she'd made a big impersonal gathering seem like a cosy afternoon-tea chat. 'It's convenient for Alastair to be married to me, and it's convenient for me to be married to Alastair.' She smiled, and her hand reached out to lightly touch his. 'Very convenient. And apart from that, we think we'll like it very, very much.'

'You're in love with him!' one of the female reporters said, on a note of discovery, and Penny-Rose refused to be disconcerted.

'Of course. Aren't you?' she asked innocently. 'I thought everybody was.'

There was general laughter and then the questioning turned back to Alastair. 'So what makes this lady special?'

Alastair took a deep breath. But suddenly his rehearsed answer went out the window because the touch of her hand on his had thoroughly unnerved him, and so had the way she'd handled this terrifying occasion. Then there was the fascination of the cotton-tail question…

All at once there was only one answer to make.

'If you can't see that, you must be blind,' he said, and there was a note of sincerity in his voice which gave Penny-Rose pause. Her laughter died.

If it were this easy…

'Where's your engagement ring?' someone asked, and she put up her hand to display a family heirloom. That rightly took the press's attention, giving them both much-needed breathing space. Things were moving way, way too fast!

And it was some rock, Penny-Rose thought, gazing down at her ring. Alastair had only produced it this morning and she wasn't accustomed to its weight on her finger. Its weight wasn't insignificant.

Pity it wasn't granite...

What had Alastair had once said? *'I never thought I'd be wining and dining a woman who'd look at rock and gasp...'*

She looked up and found his eyes on hers— and she knew he realised exactly what she was thinking. Laughter sprang between them. And something else...

'Where's your dog?' a voice called, breaking the moment. Which was just as well, because neither of them knew where the moment had been leading. Into unknown territory... She broke from Alastair's gaze to see the cameraman from Paris beaming at her from across the room. 'Where's the pup you found?'

'You mean...' Her voice wasn't quite steady. She adjusted it and tried again. 'You mean Leo?'

'Leo!' the man said, and his grin broadened. 'I might have known you'd call him something daft like that.'

The rest of the press gallery were fascinated.

'He was a stray,' the cameraman explained to the room in general. Maybe he was giving away a scoop, but it was he and only he who had the pictures from Paris. Generating interest would do no harm at all. 'The lady rescued him.'

That had everyone enthralled—as did the looks that were being exchanged between Alastair and Penny-Rose. A love story and a rescued dog... Well, well. This, then, was the human-interest story they'd craved.

Readers didn't want to hear about a marriage of convenience. Readers wanted romance— and, amazingly, it seemed as if it was romance they were being given.

'Can we see your dog?'

Penny-Rose raised her eyebrows at Alastair and he gave an imperceptible nod. Anything to get the spotlight off them, his eyes told her.

She knew exactly how he felt. 'No flash-lights, then,' she said sternly, and escaped Leo-wards.

'Is it true Miss O'Shea is a stone-waller?' she heard as she left the room.

'Of course it is,' Alastair replied. 'It's an un-usual occupation, but you have to agree that Miss O'Shea is an unusual woman.'

'You've never met anyone like her?'

'Why do you think I'm marrying her?' was the last thing she heard as she fled.

With Leo in her arms, she managed to regain her composure—sort of.

'Isn't he gorgeous?' she demanded of the room full of cynical, case-hardened reporters. Leo was clean—almost—but he was bandaged, he'd lost a heap of hair, one ear was torn and his rib cage protruded for all to see.

But Penny-Rose had decreed he was gorgeous, and there wasn't a person there who would have disagreed.

'Do you like the dog, too?' someone rounded on Alastair, and he managed a grin. The dog... Oh, right. The dog. He'd been looking at the lady.

'I like the dog.'

But he was still looking at the lady.

'This is seeming more and more like a love match,' someone whispered. This was suddenly a very different marriage to the one the press had expected.

Penny-Rose sat by Alastair's side and fielded questions with aplomb—without the least hint of shyness and uncertainty. And she glowed. Nestled on her lap, her disreputable pup wagged his tail and licked her face, then shifted to lick Alastair's face in turn. Alastair pushed the shaggy face away, but it was a very half-hearted push.

'He likes it,' a reporter whispered to a colleague. 'Hell!'

'We have headlines,' another said. 'A royal romance!'

'Followed by a royal marriage,' her colleague agreed. 'All at once, I can't wait!'

There was one more question to ask. A reporter had checked his notes. 'It says here that your name is Penelope,' he said to Penny-Rose. 'But you've been introduced as Rose. Will you be Princess Penelope?'

'No,' Alastair butted in before she could get a word out. 'She'll be Princess Rose.'

Princess Rose...

Penny-Rose looked at him with eyes that were suddenly bright with unshed tears. Princess Rose...

It might be too darned formal—but in that one unguarded moment he'd spoken her name almost as if he loved her!

'Have you seen the newspapers?'

Belle's voice woke Alastair from sleep. He'd spent the night on interminable paperwork and just before dawn he'd fallen into a troubled sleep where Rose and Leo had mingled with uncertain duty. An hour later the phone had rung.

'How could you humiliate me like this?' Belle's voice was as shrill as he'd ever heard it. 'Our friends know this is a marriage of convenience, but this...' She took a deep breath. 'This is disgusting!'

'What's disgusting?' Alastair's heart sank. Uh-oh.

'Every newspaper has these headlines... Royal Wedding. Prince Finds His Cinderella...' She seemed to be sorting newspapers as she spoke and he could hear as she tossed them aside. 'They're dreadful.'

'You knew this was going to happen,' Alastair ventured, still not sure what the problem was. 'It was a mutual decision to do this.'

'Yes, but I didn't know this would happen. Alastair, these pictures... You're sitting on the pavement in Paris, she's cuddling a dog and you're *hugging her*. And there are knickers and bras lying everywhere, and some sort of night-gown that only a slut—'

'Hey, hang on...' But he was in trouble. He knew it.

'You look as if you love her!'

And there was the nub of the matter. Alastair closed his eyes, exhaustion washing over him in waves.

'I don't love her,' he told Belle, making his voice as firm as he could. 'She was nearly hit by a car. The dog *was* hit. They were distressed and shaken. I carried both of them off the road and—'

'And you were stupid enough to be photographed.'

Silence.

Alastair thought that through and he didn't like it. He didn't respond, and after a moment of silence Belle decided that maybe she'd gone too far.

'Are you still there?'

'I'm here.' He let the weariness creep into his voice and she heard that, too.

He could hear her rethink. She was playing for a major prize here. It might be wise to draw back.

'Then can I tell my friends it was an accident? That you were playing the hero for a moment—nothing more?'

'I hope you don't tell your friends anything,' he retorted. 'Belle, you know how much is at stake. The marriage has to seem like it's permanent.'

The silence was from Belle's end now.

'I hate it,' she said at last, and Alastair nodded. So did he. Didn't he?

'But, Belle, if we back out now...'

'We'll lose everything.' She was still focussed on that ultimate prize, he realised, and it was giving her pause. 'I don't want that.'

'So what do you want me to do?'

'Act formally,' she ordered. 'These photos make you look ridiculous. Like a schoolboy with a crush.'

'I'll see what I can do,' he told her, and then he said his goodbyes—as formally as she intended that he act when Rose was around—and he tried for sleep again.

It didn't work.

Formal?

Formal and Rose didn't make sense!

Formal and Belle made sense, but he wasn't marrying Belle.

He was marrying Rose.

The thought suddenly made the thought of sleep impossible.

The next few weeks passed in a blur. There was so much to be done!

Marguerite came down with influenza and retired to bed. 'It must be from too much excitement,' she told her son, and Alastair thought of how much effort his mother had gone to in the past couple of months and felt guilty to the core. He couldn't load her with anything else.

Penny-Rose's knowledge of what was needed for a royal wedding could be written on the palm of one hand. The organisation therefore fell to Alastair, dredging up memories of relatives' weddings in the past.

Finally he located and re-employed the man who'd acted as his uncle's social secretary. He was a godsend, but he wasn't enough.

There were wedding organisers, caterers, state officials—everyone had to put their oar in. Almost the whole principality had to be invited and the production looked bigger than *Ben Hur*!

'Can't we just elope?' Penny-Rose asked as she saw the lists. Every night when she came in from her stone-walling there were more decisions to be made. She did what she could, but the look of exhaustion on Alastair's face was making her feel dreadful.

'It's a State wedding,' Alastair sighed and raked his hand through his hair. 'To be honest, I never imagined it'd get so out of hand. Every politician, every person with any clout, any deserving local…everyone would be offended to their socks if not invited.' He gave a twisted smile. 'It's made use of the chapel unthinkable. There's simply not room. The big marquee has to come all the way from Paris.' He shook his head. 'At least...'

He paused, and she prodded him to continue. 'At least?'

'At least I'll only have to do this once,' he admitted. 'Belle and I will have a simple civil affair.'

'Well, bully for you and Belle.' But she said it under her breath. Alastair was back concentrating on his lists.

She looked across the dining table at him for a long moment. The man looked almost haggard, and the urge to rise from the table and go to him was almost irresistible. To touch him on the shoulders... To massage the tension from his back and to ease the strain...

But she couldn't. She wasn't wanted.

She was simply a name in the marriage ceremony, she thought, and any female would do. His real wife would be Belle.

The thought was almost unbearable.

And dinner was finished.

'Goodnight, Alastair,' she said softly, but he didn't look up from his interminable lists. He was blocking her out.

She pushed back her plate and quietly went back to her living quarters.

Back to Leo.

'He's driving himself into the ground,' she told her little dog. 'As well trying to make everyone happy with the wedding, the estate management's a mess, and he's also trying to keep his architectural projects going. The thing's impossible.'

But he had no choice. The only thing he could give up was his architecture.

'And he can't do that because that's what he is,' she continued. 'An architect.'

Leo wagged his tail in agreement and she gave a rueful smile.

'You understand. He's an architect. Not a prince.'

As Penny-Rose was a stone-waller—not a princess.

'So you and I keep to ourselves, Leo' she murmured. 'We're not wanted. I'm just a name on a marriage certificate.

'For now...'

Penny-Rose might have gone back to Leo, but her presence stayed on with the man she intended to marry, an insistent consciousness that followed him everywhere.

He hadn't said goodnight. He'd been a bore.

But if he'd looked up, he might have said— he would have said, Help me with this. And she'd have stayed and sat beside him and the smell of her would have permeated his consciousness even more and...

And he wouldn't have been able to keep it formal. As he must!

So he'd let her go back to her dog, and he'd gone back to his paperwork, and his exhaustion and sense of confusion deepened by the hour.

He saw her again at breakfast—briefly. They were curt with each other, as formal as Belle would have wanted. Then he saw her from a distance during the day.

It was strange how often his eyes strayed to where the new west wall was gradually taking shape.

Because there'd be his intended bride, filthy and happy, chipping away at stones with Leo scrabbling in the dust beside her. Woman and dog were inseparable and Alastair had to fight an almost irresistible urge to join them.

But... 'Keep it formal,' Belle had demanded, and it was the only sensible thing to do.

Formality increased as the wedding grew closer. It was the only safe barrier. But unknown to Alastair, Penny-Rose was learning more and more about the castle and its workings.

And finally she had to break through Alastair's barriers to use it.

'Henri has bunions,' she informed him as they sat down to dinner a week before the wedding. Marguerite was still keeping to her room—her flu had left her worryingly frail—so Alastair and Penny-Rose dined alone. Formally. But for once Penny-Rose was breaking the ice. 'You should do something about it,' she told him.

Bunions... Alastair frowned. Henri... 'Did you say bunions?'

'I certainly did.' She attacked the last of her salmon with vigour, and as the butler came in to clear the plates, she beamed up at him. 'That was great, Henri. Can you tell Claude that we loved it?'

'Certainly, M'selle. Cook will be delighted.' The elderly man beamed, with a smile that left Alastair in no doubt that Rose was twisting his staff around her little finger. Henri was searching to please her now. 'Claude has made you something called lamingtons for dessert,' he told her. 'He bought a book on Australian cooking, just to make you feel at home.'

Smiling, the butler carried away his plates, and Rose turned back to Alastair as if her point had been made.

'See? He's limping, and it's getting worse.'

'I hadn't noticed,' Alastair confessed, and she smiled her royal forgiveness. If he could be regally formal, then so could she.

'No. That's because you're busy. But I did. The servants talk to me, so I can find out what's wrong.'

He'd noticed that. Often he heard laughter and it'd be Rose and the housekeeper or Rose and a kitchen maid or Rose and the gardener...

And more and more, he felt shut out.

Now, as Henri reappeared bearing a tray of...lamingtons, for heaven's sake, Alastair directed his attention to his butler's feet.

Sure enough, the man was limping.

'Rose says you need time off to have your feet attended to,' he said ruefully. 'Why didn't you tell me? I'm not a slave-driver.'

'I never thought you were,' Henri said with dignity. 'But if it was *your* workload we're talking about, I might agree. You drive yourself too hard, M'sieur.'

'I don't.'

'You do.' Henri paused and then relented. 'But if I may say so, M'sieur, it's a pleasure to work with you. You've been a breath of fresh air in the castle.' He beamed at the pair of them. 'You and M'selle Rose.'

Especially M'selle Rose, his smile said.

'Thank you,' Penny-Rose said faintly, and Henri's beam widened.

'It's my pleasure. So my bunions can stay as they are, thank you very much,' he declared. 'Take time off with your wedding in a week? No, M'sieur. Tomorrow Marie and I intend to attack the marital suite.' His eyes grew misty at the thought. 'It's forty years since your uncle brought his bride home. That marriage didn't last, but…if I may say so, that wedding was an arranged match. Not a match as this is going to be. Oh, no!'

And he limped back to the kitchens, leaving them staring after him in astonishment.

'He thinks it's real,' Alastair said, and Penny-Rose concentrated on her lamington.

'Then I guess we've succeeded.' It took an effort, but she didn't look at him. 'Have a lamington. They're delicious.'

He took a bite of a chocolate-and-coconut-covered square, but his mind wasn't on his lamington.

'What have you been telling them?'

Her eyes widened at that. 'Me? What do you mean?'

'This is a marriage of convenience,' he said heavily. 'I thought it was obvious, but the staff don't believe it.'

'Maybe they don't want to believe it,' she said gently. 'The staff have had a rough time, with the old prince's failing health and then Louis. Maybe they're looking for stability.'

'That doesn't depend on a stable marriage.'

'Of course not.' She lifted another lamington and took a bite, then surveyed it with care. 'I guess Henry the Eighth had quite a stable household.'

'Henry the Eighth?'

'The one with six wives,' she told him.

'Hey!' That was a bit much. 'I only want two.'

'Very moderate, I call it,' she agreed equitably. 'And there's been no suggestion at all of anyone getting their heads chopped off.' She chuckled across the table at him, and it was all he could do not to drop his lamington.

Hell! Things were getting seriously out of hand.

'Rose…'

'These lamingtons are great,' she enthused. 'Maybe we should honeymoon in Australia so we can eat more. I could introduce you to pav-lovas and Vegemite sandwiches and pie float-ers...'

'Pie floaters?'

'Pies in pea soup,' she explained, and he shuddered.

'If you don't mind, I'll stick to our cuisine. But that reminds me. Our honeymoon...'

'Sorry?'

'The press are expecting us to honeymoon.'

'They can expect all they like. I haven't fin-ished my wall.'

'Oh, for heaven's sake...' His pent-up emo-tions overflowed and he thumped the table. 'Rose, will you take this seriously?'

'You don't want me to take it seriously.'

'I...'

'It's a mock marriage,' she told him. She rose and gave him a mock curtsey. 'Pardon me, Your Serene Highness, but there's nothing se-rious about our marriage at all. So I'm not go-ing on a honeymoon anywhere. Sorry, Alastair, but I'm going up to say goodnight to your mother.' Then she flashed her infectious grin at him. 'Stop worrying. Go and design a mansion for someone and stop thinking of weddings. You're getting paranoid.'

And before he could stop her, she'd come around the table and kissed him, very lightly, on the top of his head. It was a teasing kiss—perfunctory and light-hearted.

There was no reason at all for him to put a hand to his forehead.

And for him to leave his hand there for a good three minutes after she'd left the room.

CHAPTER EIGHT

'I HAVE a surprise for you,' Marguerite told her.

It was four days before the wedding. The castle was a hive of activity, and with the invasion of so many strangers, Penny-Rose had grudgingly conceded to stop her walling.

She was feeling like a pampered but caged pet, but at least time with Marguerite was productive. The effects of her influenza were dragging on. Marguerite was wan and listless, she spent most of her day in bed and she had everyone worried.

But she was still scheming.

'I've had the most wonderful plan,' she told Penny-Rose. 'For your honeymoon.'

'We're not having a honeymoon.' Penny-Rose glanced up as Alastair entered the room. 'Tell her, Alastair. We don't want a honeymoon. Just a well mother-in-law.'

'That's all we want.' Alastair crossed the room and gave his mother a kiss. 'Dr Barnard was here earlier. What did he say?'

'Just more rest.' His mother sighed her exasperation. 'You can't expect anything else at my age.'

'That makes you sound as if you're ninety instead of only just seventy,' Penny-Rose retorted. She grinned. 'Madame Beric says all you need is a good tonic. She makes poor M'sieur Beric drink some foul potion full of aniseed and all sorts of horrible herbs and spices that she swears will cure anything from warts to ingrown toenails. Do you want me to get you some?'

'I don't think so,' Marguerite said faintly.

'Are you missing Paris?' Alastair demanded, sitting down on her bed. His mother had a lovely apartment near the Seine. She'd dropped everything to come here when Louis had died and she hadn't been home since. 'You've been doing so much—'

'I've hardly done anything,' his mother cut in.

'You have. Without your organisation this household would be a mess. But you must miss your friends.'

'I'll go back to Paris after I see you safely married,' she told him, and Penny-Rose gave her a strange look.

'Don't you want to go back to Paris?' she asked, feeling her way. 'Is that the problem?'

'I do...'

'You don't like it here?'

'I love it here,' Marguerite confessed.

Leo, bored with sitting on the settee with his owner, jumped down and nosed over to the bed. He leapt onto the covers and curled into the crook of Marguerite's arm.

'Maybe we could buy you a pup to keep you company,' Penny-Rose suggested, and Marguerite's face stilled.

'I don't need a dog.'

'Do you have many friends in Paris?'

Alastair frowned. Was this any of Rose's business?

But Marguerite was sighing, preparing to open up to Penny-Rose as she never talked to him.

'I only moved to Paris after my husband died. But I have...I have a beautiful apartment. Belle decorated it for me.'

Oh, great. She could imagine. A big, elegant apartment, modern and chic and sterile as hell. 'But not company?'

'I don't know many people yet...'

'Then move back here,' Penny-Rose said cheerfully. 'Decide to stay here permanently.'

She cast a quick glance at Alastair and saw she had his approval. 'Leo and I need company. It'd be great.'

'That'd be lovely dear, but…'

'But?'

Marguerite looked at her son, and then looked away. 'It'd be worse,' she said softly. 'I'd stay for twelve months and then you'd leave and Belle would come. And Belle and I don't…don't get along.'

'Belle likes you,' Alastair protested, but Marguerite shook her head.

'Belle's a woman who can't share. Whereas Penny-Rose…' She smiled fondly at her future daughter-in-law. 'Penny-Rose even shares her dog.'

'Certainly, if it means I can get a night's sleep without someone scratching his hindquarters in my face.' Penny-Rose grinned. 'So, yep, I'm extraordinarily generous, and willing to be more so. Stay with us.'

'No.' Marguerite shook her head. 'As soon as the wedding's over, I'll return to Paris.'

'If you're better,' Alastair growled, and she nodded.

'I'll be better. For your wedding I must be.' Her scheming look reappeared. 'But speaking of weddings, I was telling Penny-Rose when you came in. I have a surprise.'

'I don't trust your surprises,' Alastair said cautiously, and his mother flashed him her most innocent of looks.

'That's a dreadful thing to say. As if I'd do anything you mightn't like.'

His look of foreboding deepened. 'What have you done?'

'It's my wedding present to you both. I've booked you a honeymoon.'

'A honeymoon...' Alastair took a deep breath and looked sideways at Rose. 'We're not going on a honeymoon.'

'Of course you are,' his mother said, turning business-like. 'Everyone needs a honeymoon, and you're looking grey with exhaustion. Isn't he, Penny-Rose?'

Penny-Rose could only agree. 'Yes, but—'

'There you are.' Marguerite beamed. 'She agrees. And I'll bet Penny-Rose has never been on a decent holiday in her life. Have you, dear?'

'No, but—'

'You're not refusing to take your wife on a holiday?' Marguerite demanded of her son. 'Especially as it's already booked.' She shifted Leo to retrieve a handful of pamphlets which had been lying on the coverlet. 'These came with this morning's post. Don't they look wonderful?'

Penny-Rose looked at what she was holding up—and was caught.

'Koneata Lau...'

'It's the most beautiful resort in the world,' Marguerite told her. 'It's part of Fiji, but it's a tiny cluster of separate islands, and you book your own island. This is the one I've booked for you.'

She opened a pamphlet to poster size, and a vision of sparkling seas, palm trees, golden beaches and tiny thatched cottages caught Penny-Rose's imagination like nothing else could have.

A beach...

'I've never been to the beach,' Penny-Rose whispered before she could stop herself. 'Not properly. Not to swim. Not to stay.'

'You've never been to the beach?' asked Marguerite in surprise.

'None of us has,' she confessed. 'We lived a hundred miles inland and there was never money or time for holidays.' She took a deep breath and pushed the thought away.

'But no. Marguerite, it looks gorgeous, and thank you, but no. Honeymoons aren't for crazy marriages like ours.'

She flashed an uncertain glance at Alastair. A honeymoon would be pushing him too far and too fast, she thought. She had every intention of trying to make this marriage work, but this was a bit much.

'Besides, there's Leo,' she added, as if that clinched it. 'I couldn't leave him.'

But Marguerite had an answer for that. 'Henri and I will look after Leo as if he's our own,' she said, scratching a floppy and adoring ear. 'The staff are besotted by this dog of yours.' They were, too. In the weeks since his arrival, Leo had crept around the collective castle hearts like a hairy worm.

But that wasn't the issue here. The honeymoon was.

Beaches... Palm trees... A honeymoon with Alastair... It was a fantasy. Nothing more. But it was *some* fantasy.

She had to get away from these brochures!

'My sisters and brother will be here tomorrow,' she told them, and she couldn't stop her voice from sounding a trifle desperate. 'I can hardly get married and leave them to fend for themselves. It wouldn't be fair.'

'You intend to entertain your siblings on your honeymoon?' Marguerite was aghast.

'This is their holiday.' Penny-Rose looked at Alastair, but his face gave nothing away. This was up to her. 'They…they work hard, too, and Alastair's offer of a trip here is unbelievable.' She tilted her chin and ignored Alastair's silence. 'It'll be fun, showing them around.'

'You can hardly take your family sightseeing when you're just married,' Marguerite said, shaking her head. Beside her, Alastair's face didn't reveal one hint of what he was thinking, and it was starting to make Penny-Rose nervous.

But she had to be firm. For both of them. She set her chin in a manner both Alastair and his mother were starting to know. 'Alastair will have work to do, and we don't intend to hang in each other's pockets.' Then she cast one more wistful glance at the posters. One last look! 'So no. Thank you very much, but no.'

She rose and managed a smile at both of them, albeit a shaky one.

'I'll leave you to each other's company. I…have things to do.'

Only, of course, she didn't.

She just needed to get away from the strange expression on Alastair's face.

It was an hour later that Alastair found her.

Strangely unsettled, Penny-Rose had headed

up to the battlements. Now she sat on the parapets, hugging her knees and staring out over the countryside below.

Thinking of beaches. And hopeless marriages.

And Alastair!

He found her there. She hadn't heard him climb the stairs, and for a moment he stood in the sunshine and watched her face as she stared out away from him.

She looked bleak, he thought. And why not? She'd spent her life denying herself, and here she was denying herself again.

'I've never been to the beach...'

That one phrase had been enough to give him pause. When she'd left, Alastair had stood with his mother, staring down at the pamphlets.

He had so much...

So would she, he'd told himself. In a year she could afford to go to any beach she wanted.

But...he wouldn't be with her to see.

She'd never been to the beach.

She asked for so little. She wouldn't have entertained the idea of this marriage if it hadn't been for her family and the villagers, he knew, and the thought of her denying herself this was suddenly unbearable.

'Isn't there any way you can organise things and go?' his mother had asked at her most wistful, and he'd looked down at her with suspicion. It had been her wheedling tone.

'Just because you're sick...'

'No, dear. Just because Penny-Rose needs you.' She had hesitated. 'You know, the estate's almost at the stage where it'll run itself. Once you're married, there'll be funds for everything. Your new secretary knows the running of the place. When the wedding's over he can take over with ease.'

'And my architecture?'

'No one's indispensable,' she'd said meekly. 'And you only marry once.'

'Mother...'

'Sorry.' She'd peeped a smile at him. 'But that's what the world needs to think. And they'll think it very odd if you don't honeymoon. It would give Penny-Rose so much pleasure, and I've already booked it...'

Her voice had faded, but her expression had stayed wistful.

It had been more than a man could stand. He'd taken the pamphlets and had gone to find Rose. And now he'd found her...

Leo was sitting by her side, his doleful expression matching hers. The pup looked up at

Alastair as he appeared, and the look of reproach he gave him was almost enough to make him laugh. Good grief. You'd have sworn the dog knew!

He crossed to where she was sitting. 'Rose...'

She glanced up, and then looked back out to the river. Fast. 'I'm sorry,' she told him, without looking up at him again. 'I didn't know your mother was planning anything so dire.'

'As dire as a honeymoon?' He sat beside her. Archers had once waited up here for the Vikings to sail up the river to loot and pillage. It was hard to imagine anything so dreadful on a day like today. The sun was warm on their faces and below them the river drifted dreamily on.

'I've never been to the beach...'

'I've just been on the phone to Koneata Lau,' he said.

'Cancelling things?' For the life of her she couldn't keep the desolation out of her voice. 'That's good.'

'No. Confirming them.'

She swung around to face him, disbelief and hope warring within.

Disbelief won.

'We can't.'

'We can.'

Hope flared again, but died just as fast. 'No. It's not possible.'

'If I can, why can't you?' He ruffled Leo's shaggy ears and grinned. 'The only problem that I can see is Leo, and I've fixed that. Henri is having his bunions attended to on the day after the wedding. He'll therefore have two weeks' enforced rest, during which he'll watch daytime television with Leo on his chest. And Madame Henri will dice fillet steak for your pup every night.'

'Alastair…' Rose was half laughing, half exasperated. 'You know I can't. It's a gorgeous offer, but…'

'But what?'

'My sisters and brother…'

'That's what I need to talk to you about,' Alastair took her hands and pulled her to her feet.

Which was maybe a mistake. Her breasts pressed against his chest and, as his hands gripped hers, the texture of her hands and the closeness of her body was doing something really strange.

But he didn't know what.

Just tell her what you need to tell her and then get out of here, he thought desperately. Now.

And somehow he made his voice work.

'You're doing this for your family,' he told her. 'Marrying me. But when you said, "I've never been to the beach", I thought, They won't have either. And they're probably just as deserving as you.'

'But—'

'Shut up and listen, Rose,' he said kindly. 'This is the plan. Your brother and sisters arrive tomorrow. They can have a couple of days looking over the castle. We marry on Thursday. And on Friday the five of us get on a plane and head for Fiji. The press will think your family is going home. Koneata Lau is renowned for its privacy—photographers are shot on sight. The five of us can have a very good time.'

'The five of us…'

'All of us. The very best honeymoons are crowded,' he said, smiling. 'What do you say?'

'Oh, Alastair…' He'd taken her breath away.

All her life she'd wanted to give her family a holiday. She'd struggled but so had her siblings. Nothing was easy for a family as in debt as they were.

And to take them all to Koneata Lau!

Penny-Rose couldn't resist it. Not when it wasn't just for her. But... All sorts of possibilities were opening up before her.

'Your mother,' she whispered, starry-eyed. 'Alastair, your mother could come, too.'

'Yeah, and my butler could do with a break, and Bert and his team would build great sandcastles.' He grinned. 'No.' Then he relented. 'Actually, I asked my mother, but she refused. She's probably right when she says that a long plane flight would be too much for her.'

'If only she were well...'

'We'll get her well. After our honeymoon we'll pressure her to stay here and give her a real break. But meanwhile, the thing that could give her real pleasure is if we agree to her plan. What do you say, Rose? Can I take you—and all your family—on a honeymoon to die for?'

'Oh, Alastair...'

It was too much. She looked up at him, her eyes shining, and suddenly, before he knew what she was about, she'd stood on tiptoe to kiss him.

It had been intended as a kiss of gratitude— nothing more. But she was emotional, close to tears, and she let her feather-light kiss stay on his lips for just a fraction of a second too long.

Because somehow it became not a feather-light kiss.

In fact, feather-light suddenly didn't come near it.

Beneath the surface, a feeling of warmth and empathy had begun to flow between them, a feeling as powerful as it was real.

They'd started this mad escapade as a business proposition. What had passed between them over the last few weeks had made them friends. And now it was shifting past that, to something deeper.

It had already shifted for Penny-Rose—she knew what she was feeling—but Alastair had no idea. He'd let her lips touch his and he'd expected a soft brush of mouth against mouth. Nothing more. What he received was an electric charge that nearly blew him away.

A surge of wanting engulfed him that was so powerful—so all-engulfing—that his hands moved up instinctively to steady her. As if she could somehow feel it too and be hurt by it...

So it was natural that his hands held her—steadied her and pulled her even closer into him—and the linking of their lips forged an even stronger tie.

Dear heaven...

The taste of her... The feel of her...

He'd never felt like this, he thought dazedly.
It was as if her body were merging into his, and
there was a sweetness about her that he could
hardly believe. She was so innocent and she
was lovely and...

She was his for the taking!

She was to be his wife!

For a whole minute he gave himself up to
the exquisite sensation of savouring her touch.
Of believing that something could come of this.
Something magical—that he could let himself
love.

That in four days' time he could marry this
woman and take her to him and have her for
ever. That he could let this sensation run where
it would, letting it take its own sweet course
and be damned with the consequences.

The kiss grew deeper. Neither could break
the moment—break the contact. It was too precious. Too infinitely valuable.

It was as unexpected as it was magical.

'M'sieur...'

The voice came from below, echoing up toward the open door of the battlements. Henri
must have seen Alastair come up and was calling for him. 'M'sieur, are you there?'

With his feet, it would have been agonising for the old butler to climb the spiral staircase, but they heard the heavy tread as he started.

It was enough.

Penny-Rose broke away. For one long moment Alastair still held her, his hands on her arms and his gaze locked on hers. Their eyes reflected mutual confusion, mutual need.

But...

'I'm coming, Henri,' Alastair called, halting the man before he could do himself any damage. 'What is it?'

'Your friend from Paris is on the phone,' Henri announced. He didn't need to say more. The staff hadn't taken to Belle, and Henry used the same words and inflection every time she rang. *Your friend from Paris...*

Belle. It had to be. As usual, her timing was impeccable.

They both knew who it was, and the moment Henri spoke it was as if Belle had planted herself firmly between them. Alastair let his hands fall.

'I'm...I'm sorry,' he managed, and Penny-Rose shook her head. It needed only that. An apology.

'Don't be. I had no business to kiss you.'

'I never meant—'

'Of course you didn't.'

He looked at her uncertainly. 'It was just…
I was worried about my mother and—'

'Don't explain things to me, Alastair,' she
said gently. Because he couldn't.

Penny-Rose had to let him off the hook. He
was confused and angry with himself. She
could see that. He'd broken his unwritten rule.

This hadn't been a kiss that could be forgotten. It had been very much more.

Penny-Rose knew how much more.

But Alastair would have to discover it for
himself.

Talk about avoidance! If two people didn't
want to see each other, a castle was the perfect
home, and over the next twenty-four hours a lot
of avoidance took place.

Not deliberately, of course. Never that. But
if Penny-Rose happened to be visiting
Marguerite and Alastair decided to do the same,
he'd hear her voice on the other side of the door
and suddenly think of an urgent task down in
the offices. Or there was a cow in trouble in the
river pasture that he felt sure his farm manager
needed a hand with—and it just happened to be
dinner-time when it happened.

Or he'd be eating his leftover dinner in the kitchen and hear Henri and Rose walking down the passage toward him—and suddenly he'd had enough to eat. He was no longer hungry.

This was going to be some marriage if he couldn't face the girl!

'Keep it formal,' Belle had said, and he knew he had to do just that. Anything else was the way of madness.

He was *not* going to lose his head like a stupid schoolboy. He was not exposing himself to the pain he'd known when he'd lost Lissa. And what he'd felt for Lissa seemed pale to how he could love—

No! Stupid thought.

Keep it formal. Or keep away entirely.

For twelve months?

He could only try.

It was madness, Penny-Rose thought bleakly to herself as she tried for sleep that night. Loving and marrying without being loved in return?

For the first time she let herself think what would happen if her loving didn't work. What if nothing came of it but cold formality and divorce after twelve months?

'I could go nuts,' she told Leo. 'Seriously, peculiarly nuts.

'Or maybe I am already. Maybe I was nuts to agree to this wedding.

'And now a honeymoon.'

But she wasn't backing out. No way.

And money didn't enter the equation at all.

'He's a dish, but he's awfully formal.' Twenty-four hours into their visit her siblings were ready to pronounce judgement. 'Why doesn't he lighten up a little?'

'He's a prince. He's supposed to be formal,' Penny-Rose retorted, and got howled down for her pains.

'I suppose he wears a crown to bed.' It was Heather, ever the impertinent one. She chuckled, bouncing on her sister's gorgeous bed where they'd retired to gossip. 'What does he wear to bed, by the way? Gold pyjamas?' And then, as Penny-Rose turned an interesting shade of pink, her sister homed in like a bee to honey. 'You mean you don't know?' Her jaw dropped in amazement. 'You're engaged to be married and you don't know what he wears to bed?'

'Maybe he doesn't wear anything to bed,' Elizabeth butted in, and Penny-Rose sighed. Honestly, her sisters were incorrigible.

'Do you two mind? Mike's here.'

'Michael's sixteen years old and sixteen-year-olds know more than you do,' Heather retorted. 'I'll bet!'

It was Mike's turn to blush, but still he grinned.

'Does he lighten up?' he persisted. Accompanying Penny-Rose, Alastair had met them off the plane. He'd been welcoming and pleasant but distant, and as soon as they'd reached the castle he'd excused himself, saying Rose needed time with her family. They'd hardly seen him since.

'He's busy,' Penny-Rose said. 'He has a wedding to organise the day after tomorrow, and it's getting to him.'

But the question stayed the same. 'Does he lighten up?'

'He does.'

'If you say so.' Heather was fidgeting with her fingers. Finally she found the courage to say what needed to be said. 'Love, you're not just doing this for the money, are you? For...for us?'

If ever there was a time to admit that this was a marriage of convenience, this was it. But Penny-Rose gazed around at the anxious faces of her family and found she couldn't do it. They were obligated to her enough, she thought. It wasn't fair to make the debt deeper.

'Stoopid, why would I—?'

'You would.' Heather sounded seriously perturbed. 'I know you would. It's been getting harder and harder for us all to stay at uni, and the burden's been heaviest on you. But I can leave. I can defer for a couple of years.'

'You'd never go back.'

'I would.'

'The odds are against it.' Penny-Rose spread her hands. 'I love stone-walling and that's what I'm doing. We're all doing what we want. So…you're going to be a doctor, Liz will be an architect and Mike will be the world's greatest engineer.'

'But…' Heather was still threading her fingers. 'Not if it means you're making an unhappy marriage.' Her chin lifted and her eyes met her sister's. Really, they were very alike. 'Do you love him?' she asked directly.

And there was only one answer to that.

'Yes, I do,' Penny-Rose said, in a voice that left no room for doubt.

And how could she doubt? Marriage to Alastair? It was what she wanted, even more than stone-walling.

But what was she being offered?

Not a proper marriage. A marriage of convenience.

'Of course I love him,' she said, even more strongly. 'And how can I want any more than that?'

How indeed?

CHAPTER NINE

AND then there was the wedding.

It was a wedding that Cinderella's fairy god-mother would have approved of, Penny-Rose thought dazedly. Because the magic wands were certainly out in force today.

She'd seen the plans for the ceremony taking shape but until now everything had seemed a chaotic muddle. But on her wedding morning she woke and looked out of her window, to find the mass of canvas and poles and ropes had suddenly transformed themselves into the most beautiful marquee imaginable.

The thing was huge—almost as big as the ground floor of the castle. It stretched over the river pasture. Part of it was built on a wooden platform over the river, and there were royal pennants flying gaily from each pole. The whole scene looked like something out of a me-diaeval pageant.

And the sight made her catch her breath. Up until now this wedding had been all talk. Today it was very, very real.

What on earth was she doing? Doubts crowded in from every side as she showered and left her bedroom. Help!

But who to turn to?

Her siblings were nowhere to be found—they only had three days in this magic place and they were making the most of them. Even Leo had deserted her. Confused and aimless, she wandered down to breakfast in a muddle of caterers and guests she didn't know. Then she headed outside.

Here the sense of pageant was even stronger. Carriages were drawn up by the front gates, and horses were being walked up and down in readiness. The servants were in full livery. In her jeans and T-shirt, Penny-Rose felt like someone who'd wandered onto the wrong stage.

It was someone else's stage. Someone else's life! Not hers.

Where was Leo?

And where was Alastair?

He must be as confused as she was, she thought, but he'd absented himself. Deliberately? Maybe. And maybe he should. It was supposed to be unlucky to see the bride on her wedding day.

The way Alastair was acting, it seemed it was unlucky to see the bride at all!

But he'd organised Koneata Lau. They'd have their honeymoon when they'd have to see each other.

'Yeah, it'll be a really romantic honeymoon—just me and Alastair—and Heather and Liz and Mike,' she murmured, scooting around the edges of the marquee and trying hard to settle the sick feeling in the pit of her stomach.

Think of the beach! she told herself helplessly. Koneata Lau. It was something to look forward to.

It *should* have been just Alastair and herself, alone on a tropical island.

Which would have been a waste! she acknowledged, because if Alastair had his way they'd probably stay at opposite ends of the island. It made sense to take the kids with them.

'Be contented with what you have, girl,' she muttered to herself crossly. 'Today you have a truly royal wedding.' She looked around at the marquee with pennants flying, the castle as backdrop, the liveried servants, the carriages and the horses...

'A mediaeval wedding,' she continued.

For a year!

She kicked her toes against a rock, and one corner of her mind registered that it had a very flat base and would make a great foundation stone for the wall she was building.

That was what she felt like doing, she decided. Climbing back into her overalls and heading back to her stone-walling.

'But I can't,' she told herself. 'Get back to your quarters, woman. Turn yourself into a princess. You have a prince to marry.'

'It's magic,' Heather declared as she bounced into the room an hour later. Penny-Rose's sister looked stunning in a tiny crimson suit—a minuscule leather skirt and matching jacket. Her entrance destroyed the mediaeval air in an instant.

Heather gave her sister a resounding kiss, and whirled to admire herself in the mirror. 'Thank you for not insisting on bridesmaids,' she told her, stroking her leather with sheer joy. 'I spent all my money on this and I'll love it for ever. My friends back home will die of envy.'

Penny-Rose managed a smile. 'It's great. Where...where are the others?' Where's Alastair? she'd meant to say, but she couldn't.

'Elizabeth's flirting with a distant cousin who says he's a count. A count, for heaven's sake! I could end up with a dynasty of royal relations!

And Alastair and Mike have taken Leo for a walk by the river.'

Penny-Rose took a deep breath. She might have known. Her little brother was almost overwhelmed by all of this. While her sisters thought it was exciting, Mike had been growing quieter and quieter, and to take him for a walk had been pure kindness.

Her Alastair, she thought, was the very nicest prince a girl could ever marry!

She forced her voice to stay casual, but emotion was threatening to overwhelm her. 'They'll...they'll be back on time?'

'Of course. There's hours to go.' Heather plonked herself down on the bed, and bounced. 'This is the most gorgeous bed!' She bounced again, and then focussed on her sister's face. 'Oh, stop worrying. Alastair doesn't have to get his hair done. Like you do.' Then she grinned. 'That's what I'm here for. The team are ready. Can I tell them to come up?

'The team?'

'Wait till you see what Marguerite has in store for you.' Heather giggled. 'You'll die of shock.'

Penny-Rose didn't quite die of shock but she came close. Marguerite had decreed what was necessary and into her room came hairdresser, manicurist, beautician, florist...

A fairy godmother would have been much simpler, Penny-Rose thought, dazed. As it was, she was twisted this way and that, pampered and petted, and turned into something she'd never dreamed was possible.

And an hour later, Marguerite, looking stunning herself in a blue silk suit which must have cost a fortune, carried in *the* dress.

She had tried it on just once. It had been taken away to be altered, and now it appeared again in all its shimmering glory.

The rest of the entourage stood respectfully back, the gown was slipped over her shoulders and there was a collective gasp from the entire room.

The gown was deceptively simple. It was of made of smooth ivory silk, with a scooped neckline, tiny filigree sleeves and a bodice that showed every lovely curve. Beneath the bodice, the gown clung revealingly to her hips. Then, with a rope of rich ivory braid to delineate the skirt, it flared out into fold upon fold, sweeping to the floor at the front and drifting into a lovely rich train behind.

The skirt was so heavy! Alastair's grandmother hadn't skimped when she'd had this dress made, and the hidden folds made the gown flare and swirl like magic.

Marguerite darted forward and threaded a tiny delicate diamond tiara on Penny-Rose's head. Then the florist fixed a trace of lily of the valley into her mass of tumbling curls and the hairdresser tweaked the curls this way and that, wanting just one curl to lie on the soft curve of her breast.

And that was that. Finished.

The effect was ethereal.

'And I thought my leathers were fabulous,' Heather breathed, and it broke the ice. There was a general chuckle, the beautician made one final adjustment and Marguerite stepped forward and took Penny-Rose's hand.

'Are you ready to meet your husband, my love?'

Penny-Rose met Marguerite's eyes. They were calm and steady, and they knew exactly what they were asking. And she drew in her breath. Marguerite knew!

'I...'

'I think you're ready,' Marguerite said softly. 'Oh, my dear, this is just what I always dreamed of.'

'Marguerite—'

'Now, not another word,' her soon-to-be-mother-in-law told her, and patted her hand. 'You'll spoil your make-up.'

'Or I might crack it,' she whispered, and managed a smile. But it was nonsense. The beautician had had enough sense to leave her skin flawlessly natural.

'You'll knock your husband's socks off,' Heather declared, and Penny-Rose's smile faltered. She turned and took one last, long look in the mirror. The woman who looked back at her was a fairy princess.

She'd been handed every weapon she could possibly need, she thought.

The rest of it was up to her.

Or how strong Alastair's defences could be.

She'd knock his socks off?

'That's my intention,' she murmured. 'OK, Alastair de Castaliae. Prince Alastair. Here I come. Ready or not.'

They'd decided on no formal bridal party.

'If you don't want bridesmaids, I won't have groomsmen,' Alastair had said. 'It's just as well. There's no one close enough to be an obvious best man. Whoever I ask, someone else is bound to be offended.'

And it was ridiculous, given Penny-Rose's fierce independence, that someone give her away.

So they'd decided that she'd walk up the aisle by herself, she'd have no attendants, and Alastair would carry his own ring.

Her sisters fussed around her as she arrived, but with her train arranged beautifully to sweep down the aisle behind her, they took themselves to the front row to watch her make her way to her bridegroom in solitary splendour.

And all at once, solitary splendour felt very, very lonely.

There must be a thousand people present, she thought dazedly, starting that long solemn walk as a lone trumpeter sounded.

And then she saw Alastair.

He was dressed in a soft grey morning suit—of course—and he looked magnificent. The only touch of colour was a crimson rosebud in his lapel.

A rose... The flower of love... Marguerite had chosen the flowers, and Penny-Rose carried twelve matching buds in her bouquet.

The sight, for some reason, made her feel like weeping. Red roses for her wedding day... It seemed almost a mockery.

But Alastair was watching her, and his eyes were calm and reassuring. A tiny smile creased the corner of his mouth.

Dear God, he was so…so…

So Alastair. There was no other way of describing him, because that was who he was, and she loved him so much that she felt she was close to breaking.

How could she do this? she thought wildly. She was marrying the man under false pretences. Alastair didn't want a wife who loved him to bits. He didn't even really want a wife…

Panic was suddenly close to overwhelming her.

And then she saw Michael. Her baby brother.

Alastair's promise that he'd have no attendants had gone out the window. Michael had Alastair's ring in his hand, he was wearing a morning suit to match Alastair's and the look on his face was as if he'd been handed the world.

The sixteen-year-old had flown halfway around the globe to be at his sister's wedding, but until this moment he'd been thoroughly confused by everything that was going on. Sixteen-year-olds were insecure at the best of times. Unlike Heather and Liz, he'd hated this.

But now he'd been handed a part to play, and what a part! Best man! And in his free hand— the one that wasn't holding the ring...

For heaven's sake, Mike was holding a leash. He was holding Leo!

The pup had been brushed to an inch of his life, and he'd never looked so splendid. The scars on his side were almost healed, but they were completely covered by a magnificent crimson doggy coat. He wore a studded collar, his lead was crimson suede and he beamed at the approaching bride and wagged his tail as if this entire ceremony was being put on for his benefit.

Her brother. And her dog...

Alastair had done this—for her!

She couldn't help it. Panic subsided, and despite the aura of solemnity—despite the state officials and the hundreds of people she'd never seen in her life, despite the grandeur and the fuss—she chuckled.

This would be OK.

She loved this man so much... He'd known how alone this ceremony would make her feel, so he'd done the two things that could ease her fears.

He was *some* prince!

And surely the only thing to do with a prince like this was to marry him?

And Alastair watched his bride come toward him with a feeling in his chest that was almost as close to panic as hers.

What was he doing? *Marrying?*

This wasn't real, he told himself. It was a pretence. It was a mock wedding, made for the best of purposes—to protect his tenants and to provide for their future.

In twelve months he'd let this woman go and he'd marry a sensible woman—a woman who suited his lifestyle.

Belle.

But the thought of Belle was suddenly very far away. What was real was Penny-Rose.

No! She was Rose, he told himself. For some reason it was a distinction it was important to keep. Penny-Rose was for those who loved her. Rose... Rose was to be his formal wife.

So it was Rose who was walking toward him, her eyes wide and her face determined. Despite her determination, her steps were faltering.

She was fearful, he thought. Damn, it hadn't been fair to drag her into this. Into the goldfish bowl of royalty.

But she was so beautiful she took his breath away! She was wearing his mother's dress, a dress that would have been equally beautiful a hundred years ago. She looked timeless and serene and incredibly lovely. In fact, she looked just as a princess should.

His princess.

For a year.

The time frame was suddenly gut-wrenching. But then...he saw the exact moment she registered that Mike and Leo were by his side. He saw the serenity and solemnity vanish, along with the fear. Laughter flashed into her lovely eyes, her lips twitched with pleasure and as she reached him he heard a low, lovely chuckle.

'Oh, Alastair...'

Her laughing face was raised to his and he gazed down at her for a long, long moment.

Then he calmly took her hand and smiled back.

This was suddenly very, very OK.

His princess.

Her prince.

And while the world watched, they turned together to be made one.

The wedding celebrations went on through the day and far into the night. And what a night!

Because the weather was perfect, the sides of the marquee were raised so the dance floor was partly over the river and partly over the pasture. The moon was brilliant. The night was brilliant! No one wanted to go home.

And everyone wished to dance with the bride. She was passed from one partner to another and her feet barely had time to touch the ground. Alastair was free to do as he willed.

Which was just what he wanted, he told himself, trying not to follow his new wife with his eyes. She was dancing with one of his business partners now, clasped around the waist in a manner that made him want to—

'Alastair?'

He paused as he realised who was calling. Belle...

Belle's presence had been necessary here, if only to allay gossip, and there was no reason now that they shouldn't speak.

Strange that it felt almost like a betrayal...

But Belle didn't notice. She looked very pleased with herself. 'I've been talking to Marguerite,' she announced. 'She tells me you're taking Rose's family on your honeymoon. That's a great idea.'

'It'll take the pressure off,' he agreed, still watching his wife twirling across the floor.

Then he thought about what he'd said. Why should there be any pressure?

Belle was raising one elegant eyebrow. 'Pressure? Surely you're not worried that she'll ravish you?' She wasn't worried at all. Rose was such an insignificant little thing, her tone implied, and Alastair was forced to smile.

'Of course not. I mean…having other people to share the conversation. It'll help.'

He received a blinding smile of sympathy. 'She'll bore you within a day,' Belle agreed. 'Poor darling.'

It wasn't fear of boredom that was worrying him, he decided, but if that's what Belle thought, maybe it was just as well.

'I can cope. This marriage is only for twelve months,' he reiterated, and it was as if he was reassuring himself.

'Of course it is.' Belle kissed him lightly—a gesture that was as natural as any guest congratulating a bridegroom—and then she stepped back. Their path was set and she, for one, was sure of the rightness of what they were doing. 'Secure your fortune and then we're settled for life. Off and do your duty, my darling. Just don't let the creature fall in love with you.'

The creature…

Belle hadn't meant it as it had sounded, Alastair decided as he succeeded in claiming and dancing with his lovely new wife, but the description rankled.

It rankled for the rest of the evening.

She was *not* a creature. She was his wife.

Just for a year.

His hold grew imperceptibly tighter, and his patience with other men wishing to claim her grew thin. A year wasn't very long...

'Belle's looking lovely,' she told him as the music slowed and he held her close.

'She is.' He swirled her around and smiled down into her dancing eyes. 'And so's the man you were just dancing with.'

That had her startled. 'What—lovely?'

'You might say that. He wouldn't mind. Maurice is gay.'

'Oh...' She choked on laughter. 'Are you sure?'

'No, but if he insists on wearing a pink bow-tie and matching braces he has to expect a suspicion or two.'

She choked again. 'What an ungentlemanly thing to say. You sound almost jealous, Alastair de Castaliae.'

'How could I be jealous?'

'How indeed? When you have Belle right where you want her.'

Right. She was right. He did have Belle. Sort of.

But meanwhile, he had his wife right where he wanted her.

In his arms.

They danced until dawn. Then, as they bade farewell to the last stray guest, Alastair glanced at his weary bride and felt an almost overwhelming urge to pick her up and carry her back to his castle. Further. Back to the ready and waiting bridal chamber.

Which was all very well, but he wanted a change to their plans. He wanted the door between them to be unlocked!

In days of old he could have done it, he thought savagely. If the prince were the real lord of the manor, he could have claimed this woman for twelve months—properly taken her—then discarded her and taken another.

But he couldn't think of another. He could only think of the woman by his side. He absorbed the weariness on her lovely face, the way her soft body yielded to his touch, the fragrance of her. The way she looked...

He'd never seen a woman as lovely as his wife looked tonight.

His wife?

He was going nuts, he thought. He should stop thinking like this. He must! She was just...Rose. There was no 'his wife' about it. Not really.

This was a business arrangement and nothing else.

'Tired?' he managed, and she chuckled.

'How can you doubt it? Oh, but, Alastair, it's been the most wonderful day. A day to remember for ever. And my gorgeous gown hasn't turned to rags yet.' She managed another chuckle. 'The pumpkins have stayed at bay, and I have twelve months to go before my midnight.'

She did. Twelve months. Twelve whole months. The thought was suddenly immensely cheering. She'd be with him until then, working as he worked...

The thought of her work reminded him of something important.

'I have a wedding gift for you,' he told her.

'A wedding gift...' She gazed up at him in surprise. 'There's no need. You've given me enough.'

'Not quite enough.' He smiled down at her. 'I realise I don't know you very well, so I asked Bert what you most wanted, and I've got you just that.'

'You asked Bert... Then I can't imagine,' she said faintly.

'Shut your eyes.' The dawn was just starting to break. The bride and groom had decided not to make a formal departure, which left them now at the entrance to the marquee, on the river bank and alone.

'I'll lead you,' he said softly, and he took her hand in his. 'Trust me?'

With all my heart, she thought, but she didn't say it. She merely nodded, and let herself be led.

Her wedding gift was on the other side of the castle. They made their way in the soft dawn light across the pastures of buttercups and poppies, to where the new wall was being built.

The team had finished the most urgent repairs, but there were miles of fencing yet to go. A whole year's worth of stone-walling, Penny-Rose thought happily.

And then she saw Alastair's gift.

It was a vast mound, about six feet high and eight feet square. It was wrapped in some sort of white parchment, and a vast gold bow about three feet high adorned the whole thing.

What on earth…?

'It's soap and a hand-towel,' Penny-Rose said faintly and Alastair grinned.

'Some soap! Nope. Bad guess. Try again.'

'A toaster, then?' She giggled. 'Or a casserole?' Her thoughts slipped sideways. 'We've been given so much… We'll have to keep careful notes and send everything back.'

At the end of the year…

It was a bad thought. It sobered them both. But the parcel was still in front of them, enticing in its mystery.

'Aren't you going to open it?' Alastair demanded.

'I don't think I dare.' She was eyeing it as if it might bite. 'It looks like it could be a rhinoceros.'

He grinned. 'Damn, you guessed.'

She smiled, but her smile was troubled. 'Alastair, you needn't have done this. It makes it seem…'

'Makes it seem what?'

'It makes it seem almost a proper wedding,' she whispered, and her words felt good to Alastair.

He might only have her for a year, but a year was better than nothing.

For heaven's sake, what was he thinking?

The current had caught him unawares, and he was being swept along without realising it. Which was ridiculous, he thought savagely, hauling himself back to some sort of common sense. Hadn't he made himself a vow when Lissa died? Had Lissa's death taught him nothing?

This was a marriage of convenience. Nothing more.

As was this gift to his wife. It wasn't a proper gift. It was only…

'Open it,' he said, and she cast him an uncertain glance. Something had changed.

'Open it,' he growled, and she took a deep breath. OK. Keep it formal. Concentrate on the parcel.

And what a parcel! She had to tug the vast ribbon until it floated free, and after that she had to pull aside the parchment. And inside were…

'*Copestones?*' She stood back in incredulity. 'You've given me *copestones*?'

'Bert said one of the reasons he employed you was that you were a copestone perfectionist,' Alastair said, trying not to sound *too* pleased with himself. These stones had taken a lot of organising. 'He also told me the main reason your hands are a mess is because you chip the damn things until they're perfect.'

'But otherwise they don't look good.' Penny-Rose was lifting a single stone and staring at it in disbelief. Copestones were the stones used to top and weight her wall. Chosen and chipped well, they made the wall look great—the icing on the cake! But it could take her almost half an hour to chip a stone to this shape, and on this job Bert had refused to give her the time.

'There's too much to do. We can't afford your standards here,' he'd told her. 'This is farmwork. We have a job to do and we need to be economical.'

She'd agreed, but she made them perfect anyway, working into her lunch-hours and evenings to get them right so her stones would still look magnificent in hundreds of years.

But they took so much effort, and here they were, already cut.

'How…?' She couldn't believe what she was seeing. 'How…?'

'I employed men off site,' Alastair explained. 'Bert showed them what you've been doing and said we wanted more of the same. They delivered them this morning.' As she replaced her stone, he lifted her hands and fingered her rough skin. 'So, for the next year you can go on stone-walling all you like, but the hardest bit's done.'

'Oh, Alastair...'

'It was Bert's idea.'

'It was no such thing.' She knew that much at least. Alastair must have thought of this all by himself. She thought back to the day a couple of weeks ago when he'd discovered her swearing over a gashed hand and a copestone that wouldn't cut as she'd wanted it. 'Bert wouldn't have thought of this as a gift.' She managed a wavering smile. 'Not in a million years. As a matter of fact, I think one of our toasters is his.'

'It would be.'

Silence. She carefully disengaged his hand. For some reason it was suddenly important that she do so.

A thousand copestones...

She couldn't have thought of a better wedding gift if she'd tried.

Damn, there was a tear trickling down her nose—and then another one. She wiped them fiercely away with the back of her hand, and gave a very unromantic sniff.

Which suddenly made Alastair feel very romantic indeed.

This was unreal. Standing in the dawn light, beside a mound of stones, with a woman in bridal attire... A woman who sniffed and tried to look fierce when he knew she wanted to burst into tears. And the reason for those tears? Because here was a woman who thought a pile of copestones was the greatest present...

He put a hand out to touch her, but she backed away as if she were scared of being scorched. 'No!'

'No, what?' His eyes were on hers. 'Don't you like my gift?'

'I...I do.' But Penny-Rose knew what she'd stepped back from. She knew what was close to happening. And she didn't want this man to kiss her.

Not yet. It wasn't right.

She didn't want to seduce him, she thought frantically. Nor did she want him to make love to her because she was convenient.

She wanted him to fall in love with her. As she loved him. So intensely that she ached...

'I...I have a gift for you, too,' she murmured softly, and it brought him up short. A gift...

'You don't have any money,' he said before he could stop himself, and she glared.

'Yeah, well, there are some things that can be gained without money. Like Leo.'

'Like our aristocratic dog,' he agreed. 'A gift without price.' And then his brow creased and he grinned in mock dismay. 'Oh, hell. Don't tell me. Another dog?'

'It's nothing of the kind,' she said with dignity. 'Though if I find one with just the right pedigree...'

'To match Leo's.'

'That's right.' She was relaxing again now. The moment of tension had passed. 'So...do you want to see my gift?'

'Of course I do.' He was fascinated.

'It doesn't come in a velvet box either,' she told him. 'And it's not gift-wrapped. It's no toaster.'

'Rose, there's no need to give me anything.'

'You brought the kids over for the wedding,' she said simply. 'You've given me the earth. So of course there's a need for a gift. It took me a while to figure out what, but I finally did.'

'What—?'

'Come and see.'

Once again they walked around the castle, but this time south, where pastures gave way to woodland. Here there was a small rise, looking back over the castle to the cliffs and river plains beyond. It was a place of absolute beauty. Penny-Rose had found it one day when she'd sought a quiet place to eat her lunch, and she'd been back again and again ever since.

And finally she'd asked Marguerite about it.

'My husband loved the castle,' Marguerite had said. 'In a way, he felt it was his ancestral home. And Lissa's family couldn't bear for her to be buried alone. There's a crypt for the royal family underneath the chapel, but we thought...it'd be lovely if they were buried here.'

So there were two simple gravestones, nestled among the woodland. And surrounded by flowers...

'Alastair planted them,' Marguerite had told her. 'All the flowers we both love. Wildflowers and roses and daffodils and tulips and honey-suckle and wisteria... So it'll be a mass of flowers all year round.'

The only jarring note, to Penny-Rose's mind, was the fence. They'd erected a simple wire fence around the graves to keep the cattle out, and it looked discordant in such a lovely place.

So she'd fixed it.

Alastair hadn't been here for weeks. He'd had so much on his plate he hadn't had time.

But now... He saw what she'd done before he reached the graves. His steps slowed. He walked up to the fence and he stopped and took it in.

It was the most beautiful fence he'd seen in his life. Made of simple sandstone, every stone was perfect. The fence formed a tiny fold about ten feet square, a croft where the graves were protected against the weather and against the cattle.

And the fence was built with such care and craftsmanship that the graves would be protected for a thousand years.

It was high—four feet or so—so the sturdiest sheep couldn't climb over, but there were throughstones forming a stile so one could enter.

And she'd formed smoots—narrow slits in the stone—regularly spaced, all the way along. 'To let light in, and so the woodland creatures can enjoy your garden,' she explained, watching his face with some anxiety. 'The first morning I walked up here I saw a litter of tiny rabbits munching on your buttercups. And I thought...if this was my grave that's what I'd want.'

Silence.

'I can pull it down if you don't like it,' she whispered, still anxious. 'But it was the one thing I could do for you. I know you loved your dad and you loved Lissa. And somehow this seemed right.'

It did, too.

It seemed perfect.

Alastair climbed the stile without a word. Reaching the top, he held out his hand. After the briefest of hesitations, Penny-Rose placed her hand in his and climbed the stile with him. Her wedding dress was lifted carefully over, and then they were together in the fold.

Around them, wildflowers blossomed around masses of tulips. Wisteria had been carefully restrung against the stones. As it was late spring it was losing its flowers so a carpet of soft blue petals lay everywhere, and the wild roses were just starting to bloom.

The smell of the morning was with them. The dew on the grass left a pungent fragrance where they walked, and the two simple graves lay gently side by side. Like two friends.

As they had been, Marguerite had told her. Lissa had been almost a daughter to Alastair's parents. These were Alastair's people, and it was right that they be buried together.

'Thank...thank you,' he said in a voice that wasn't too steady, and this time it was he who badly wanted to sniff. Penny-Rose heard it and managed a grin. She was still feeling distinctly sniffy herself.

Keep it practical... 'Not carrying a handkerchief?' she managed.

'They gave me a buttonhole instead.' He smiled, and plucked the crimson rose from his lapel. 'As a handkerchief it makes a very poor substitute, but here it is. What's mine is yours.'

It was a simple statement—a jest—but it hung between them like the promise of the morning to come.

Only...the morning was already here.

'We...we'd best get back to the castle,' Penny-Rose said uncertainly. 'We have a plane to catch this afternoon and we haven't had any sleep.'

'That's right.' But he couldn't keep his eyes from her. 'We have a honeymoon to begin.'

'A holiday,' she corrected him. 'You need to be really married to go on a honeymoon.'

'And we're not really married?'

She hitched her dress high. This scene was threatening to run away with her, and she wasn't ready. Alastair wasn't ready.

Seduction wasn't her scene. She was playing for keeps, so she had to be practical. Somehow.

'No, Alastair, we're not,' she told him. She looked down at Lissa's grave, and a tiny smile curved her lips. 'I hope we're becoming like you and Lissa...good friends. But that's not a basis for a marriage.'

'Lissa and I thought so.'

'Well, I'm not Lissa.' She stepped up onto the stile and stayed on the fence-top for a moment, looking down. She looked immeasurably lovely, dressed in her bridal finery, with the dawn light behind her and the carpet of wild-flowers at her feet. 'I'm me. I'm Penny-Rose. The girl who married for money. I'm your bride for a year, but just for a year, Alastair de Castaliae. So let's not forget it.'

The door between Alastair and his new bride was firmly locked.

'Goodnight,' she'd said sweetly as they'd arrived back at the castle. She'd stood on tiptoe to kiss him but it had been a fleeting kiss of farewell—nothing more. 'We only have eight hours till we catch our plane. I'm off to get some beauty sleep and I suggest you do the same.'

But how could he, when every nerve in his body screamed that his bride was just on the other side of the door?

Belle.

Think of Belle, he told himself desperately. He'd promised to marry her. That was the sort of marriage he wanted. Not...not what he could have with Rose.

And what sort of marriage was the one he envisaged with Rose? If he allowed it to become...proper.

It was the sort of marriage his mother had had, he acknowledged, because if he allowed himself to give—as Rose gave—there'd be no holding back.

And if anything happened...

As it did. As life had taught him it always did. He'd committed himself to Lissa and it had ended in tragedy.

If something like that happened again, he'd go crazy, he told himself fiercely.

But maybe he was going crazy already!

CHAPTER TEN

TAKING the kids on their honeymoon didn't make it less romantic, Alastair decided a few days later. It made it more so. After initial polite protests, the kids had agreed to accompany them. They intended to have a great time but they also intended their sister to have a honeymoon to remember for ever.

Which included romantic seclusion.

'We want to spend time with you,' both Penny-Rose and Alastair protested, but their words fell on deaf ears.

'Well, we don't want to spend time with you,' Heather declared. 'So this morning we've booked the catamarans. One each. We're having lessons and the instructor can only take three, so you guys will just have to find something else to do. Hmm. I wonder what?' She threw them a cheeky grin and disappeared.

Which left them alone. Again.

'I...I'll take a walk,' Penny-Rose said, and Alastair gazed at her in exasperation. In three days she hadn't relaxed once, and the island wasn't big enough to stay away from each other for ever.

'Can I come with you?'

She appeared to give it serious thought. As if she didn't really want to. 'I... If you like.'

'I do like.'

Of course he liked. Who wouldn't? OK, it might be unwise, but in a simple sarong, with her hair hanging free and her nose sporting a touch of sunburn, she looked almost breathtakingly lovely. What man could resist walking beside a woman like this?

Especially when that woman was his wife.

In name only!

He had to keep reminding himself of that. Ever since they'd arrived they'd been treated as being very much in love, and formality was harder and harder to maintain.

The sleeping arrangements were the hardest. There were three guest cottages on the island—gorgeous thatched bures. If Alastair and Penny-Rose had done what they'd first planned and had the island to themselves, they could have had a cottage each. But Liz and Heather had taken one and Michael another. Which left only the honeymoon suite.

The suite was gorgeous. Built right on the edge of the waves, whenever they liked they could push back the folding walls so that sea air and moonlight drifted right into the room with them. Simple but beautifully built, it was almost erotic in its design, with one enormous bed taking up over half the room.

So... The sensible plan had been to place a row of cushions down the middle of the bed.

It worked—sort of. But the trace of shadows under Rose's eyes told Alastair that she was feeling the strain almost as much as he was.

She was so near and yet so far.

She was his wife!

She was his paid companion for a year, he reminded himself harshly as they walked slowly along the sand. Nothing more. He couldn't let her any closer than this. Otherwise when it ended he'd go nuts.

Did it have to end?

Yes, he told himself fiercely. It must. Even if he was stupid enough to lose his heart, there was Belle to consider.

And it was just plain stupid to let himself lose his heart. Hadn't life taught him anything?

'Penny for them?' Penny-Rose asked, and he lifted his head with surprise. They were in the shallows, barefooted and kicking their way through the foam. Alastair was wearing his bathing trunks and nothing else. Which was just as well. Any minute now he could end up swimming.

If things became too hot...

'I beg your pardon?' He had trouble forcing his thoughts from where they'd been straying.

'Penny for your thoughts?' she repeated. 'You look away with the fairies.'

He managed a smile. 'Was I? Sorry. I was thinking of Belle.'

Penny-Rose's smile faded. Belle. Of course. She was between them all the time. 'You must miss her.'

'I... Yes.'

'This'll be hard on you both,' Penny-Rose admitted. 'Knowing how beautiful this is...' She brightened a little. 'Still, the fact that my sisters and brother are here must make it easier for her.'

'I...' Hell, concentrate! Make yourself talk sensibly, he told himself. 'It does. Belle approves of the idea.'

'I'm glad.'

But Belle had called Rose 'the creature'.

Alastair looked across at the creature in question. The soft breeze was blowing her hair into a tumble of riotous curls. The sun was warm on her face and she was lifting her nose to smell the sea.

'Isn't it gorgeous?' she breathed, and he was forced to smile his agreement.

'Absolutely.' But he wasn't talking about what *she* was talking about.

Maybe he'd better head for the water!

But beside him Penny-Rose had paused. Far out in the bay, just around the headland from where they were, she could see three little catamarans. Her siblings were having a ball. She watched for a while, and then sighed and smiled.

'I want to thank you,' she said seriously. 'Alastair, what you're doing for us...'

'I'm doing it for me.'

'I don't think you are,' she said softly. Before he could stop her she'd caught his hand and was tracing the strong lines below the wrist. 'I think you're doing this for your tenants and for Belle and for your mother—*and* for me. But maybe not for you. I'm starting to know that you don't really want to be royalty.'

'Being royalty can't hurt.' The feel of her hand was unnerving. One part of him wanted to pull away.

The other part of him wanted to move in closer.

'You dislike the publicity.'

'I... Yes.'

'It'll get worse.'

'For a while.'

'Because of our marriage?'

'I guess.'

'And the divorce at the end—there'll be a heck of a fuss.'

'I can cope.' He shrugged. A year was starting to seem a very long way away.

'I wish I could make it easier for you.'

The only way she could make things easier was to leave right now. He was starting to feel as if he was being torn in two. To have her so near...

'Come in for a swim,' he suggested, and she kicked up some water with her toes.

'I wish I could.'

He'd forgotten. Again.

She couldn't swim. He'd discovered it on the first day. The others had somehow managed to learn but his wife hadn't been so fortunate. In her tough childhood, there'd simply never been time.

And Alastair hadn't found the courage to say what he most wanted to say. That he'd teach her.

Because how could he teach her without touching her? And how could he touch her without—?

He hauled his hand away and grimaced. 'OK. You do your splashing bit and I'll do my lap stuff.'

Which was fine, he thought savagely as he stroked strongly in deep water. This way he could put some of his unused physical energy to good use. So far this holiday he must have swum for twenty miles or more. Every time things got too much for him he swam while Rose enjoyed herself in the shallows.

Did she enjoy herself?

Of course she did, he told himself. She'd never been to the beach. It was a novelty. The shallows were enough!

He was being mean!

But if he wasn't mean…that way led to disaster. Teaching her to swim… Letting her close…

Alastair paused but as he did so a movement caught his eye. Entranced, he trod water and watched.

Out past the breakers, where the waves were forming into massive, rolling swells, a pod of dolphins had come in to surf. They were darting into the sapphire crests, row upon row of them—there had to be thirty—using the force of the waves to surf gloriously toward shore.

Alastair was just far enough out to see. They were past the sand-bar which created the lagoon effect where Alastair swam and Rose paddled. Between sand-bar and the beach, the water sloped gently, meaning he had to be a hundred yards from the beach before he could swim.

And that meant Rose could hardly see the dolphins from where she was.

She'd love them. Alastair watched the sea creatures for a moment longer, and then he glanced back at Rose. She was lying full length in the shallows, letting the foam trickle through her toes. She was wearing a crimson bikini, and nothing more.

She looked blissfully happy, and very, very lovely.

But the dolphins were a sight to be seen maybe once in a lifetime, Alastair thought desperately. She should see them.

She couldn't see them from where she was. Not properly.

And there was a channel fifteen or twenty feet wide of deep water between shore and the sand-bar. That was where he'd been swimming.

Maybe she'd trust him to tow her through the deep water to where the sand-bar created a ledge, he thought. If she let him do that, then they could both see.

To have him carry her through deep water when she couldn't swim she'd have to trust him absolutely.

And suddenly there was no reason why not. And every reason why.

'Rose,' he shouted, and started over to where she lay. 'Come and see. It's magic.'

And it *was* magic. As was her trust. She lay limply in his hold, totally reliant on his strength as he carried her out to sea. And he knew how reliant she must be. The channel of deep water was maybe only fifteen feet wide, but for a non-swimmer to trust that much was no mean feat.

'Kick your legs,' he said, and felt her do just that.

Her courage was immutable. She was some lady!

But touching her, towing her strongly alongside him in the deep water with his arm holding her close...

This was an indescribable sensation!

Finally he felt the sand-bar rise underneath him, and he guided her feet so she could stand.

But then, somehow, he didn't—couldn't—quite let her go. After all, he had to guide her so she was looking toward the dolphins. And they were still near deep water, so if she fell he'd have to support her.

And she felt so good by his side. So right!

But she seemed almost unaware of the man by her side. She was totally focussed on the dolphins.

And why not? For someone who'd never been to the beach, the creatures were entrancing. They surfed and tumbled and dived, swimming for the sheer exuberance of being alive. Time after time, they darted into the waves, streaming through the sapphire waters, their bodies like glinting silver arrows, and the joy they felt was almost a tangible thing.

'They're just...they're just magic,' Rose whispered, and Alastair could only agree. It *was* magic.

The whole morning was magic. This place. The island. The dolphins, the sun on his face...

This woman!

And then, as suddenly as they'd appeared, the dolphins departed, backing out of the waves and leaping and cresting along the shoreline, around the headland and off to thrill the three younger ones on their catamarans.

'Do you think they're paid by the island management?' Penny-Rose whispered, her voice still awed, and Alastair managed a smile.

It was a wonder he could manage anything. His body was doing very, very strange things.

His head was also doing strange things!

But he had to force his voice to sound normal. 'With the price we're paying, they've probably been trained in Miami,' he told her, and then he laughed at the expression on her face. 'Nope. They were the real thing, lady. Totally wild and totally free, giving us the performance of their lives just for their pleasure. And ours.'

She closed her eyes, and he felt her take it all in. The sheer loveliness of it. The wonder.

And then she opened her eyes again and he saw that the real world had intruded. She shifted away from him—imperceptibly, but it was a shift for all that.

'Take me back to shore,' she said simply. 'Thank you for bringing me out, but it's time my feet hit the ground.'

'You should be able to swim,' he growled, and she nodded.

'Yes.' She couldn't quite keep the note of wistfulness from her voice. 'But I can't. So I need a tow. And then you can get back to your swimming.'

And all at once Alastair couldn't bear it. She asked for nothing, he thought savagely. She gave and gave and gave. If he hadn't had a damned good reason—like saving the tenants' livelihoods—for this marriage, she'd never have made it.

She wouldn't marry for profit. She wouldn't do anything for profit, he thought. Not for herself.

'Would you like to learn to swim?' he asked, and it was as if someone else were doing the asking. He hadn't meant to. Had he?

'Would I like...?'

'I can teach you.' He smiled. 'I taught Lissa.'

The name came up naturally, with no strain at all. Lissa... He'd hardly talked about Lissa since her death. He'd tried not to think of her. But now the memories came flooding back, of Alastair as a ten-year-old, holding his six-year-old cousin under the tummy and yelling, 'Kick, kick...'

And Lissa kicking so hard he'd been bruised for weeks!

He grinned suddenly, and it was as if a weight had been lifted that he hadn't known was there. The grieving had shifted imperceptibly, and the memories that remained were full of sunlight and laughter and love.

But not passion...

The passion he was learning about hadn't come into the equation, he thought as Penny-Rose watched his face. He and Lissa had been such good friends that they hadn't wanted more—or simply hadn't known that more existed. And she'd been killed before they'd found out.

And now…

Now he knew more existed. Because what he was feeling for the woman by his side was very, very different.

Hell!

But Penny-Rose was lifting her eyes to his, and the expression on her face said she understood.

She couldn't understand. How could she? It was his imagination.

'If you could teach Lissa, then you can teach me,' she said softly. 'Oh, Alastair, I'd love it.'

Thus began one of the funniest, most precious days of Alastair's life. All the rest of the morning they worked at it. Her trust was absolute, and her faith paid dividends.

'You'll do dead-man's float first,' he told her, and made her lie face down in the water. 'Lie as flat as a board and don't let yourself put your head up until I touch your shoulders.'

And she didn't. He put his hand under the flatness of her stomach and held her—supporting her totally—and the feeling it gave him was spine-tingling. She lay still and trusting, until he touched her shoulder. Then she gasped and spluttered and knelt up on the sand to laugh in sheer delight.

They did it again and again, until she was almost floating by herself. 'It feels wonderful. It feels weird.'

'It'll feel weirder. This time I'm going to lower my hand and you'll feel the water supporting you instead of me. You'll float.'

And she did! She floated as if she'd done it since childhood, and he gazed down at her beautiful body—and almost forgot to touch her shoulder! When he did, she spluttered a whole lot more as she struggled to her feet. He expected indignation but what he received instead was blazing joy.

'I floated. I floated! All by myself, I floated!'

'If I don't touch your shoulder you can decide to put your head up yourself,' he managed, laughing with her joy but trying desperately to ignore the strange feelings coursing through his body.

Penny-Rose didn't understand. 'Why would I? You'll touch me when it's time to surface. I trust you.'

He knew it. The thought was incredible. 'But...if I'm eaten by a shark...'

She grinned, delirious with sun and surf and happiness. 'Then I'll drown of a broken heart, dead-man's-floating to my doom. What a princess! people would say. Romeo and Juliet would have nothing on a scenario like that.'

He chuckled. 'Hey, there's no need to go to extremes. Dying of devotion...'

All of a sudden the lightness faded. They were standing in the shallows, looking at each other, and her words hung between them.

'I'll drown of a broken heart...'

And his.

'Dying of devotion...'

The words had been said in jest, but suddenly things weren't light at all. Things were moving fast here, changing every minute. The magnetism between them was a tangible power. It was gaining strength every second, and to resist the pull...

How was he to sleep next to her tonight? he asked himself desperately. On the other side of the mound of pillows...

Concentrate on practicalities.

'Speaking of lunch,' he said, and her look of uncertainty faded. She was starving, and passion could maybe take a back seat. It was a shame, but where he led, she'd follow. Don't push the pace...

'Now you're talking. I wonder if flake's on the menu?'

'You mean we get to eat shark before it eats us? How very wise.' He managed a grin and glanced at his watch. 'It'll be on the table right now. Race you up to the dining room, Rose O'Shea.'

'It's Penny-Rose de Castaliae to you, sir,' she said meekly, and while he took that on board she gained so much of a head start that she beat him to lunch, hands down.

And by nightfall she could swim. Not very far, but she could manage half a dozen strokes before she had to surface, and she was so proud of herself she was threatening to burst.

'I can swim, I can swim,' she crowed at dinner, and her sisters and brother looked on with wonder.

'You sound like a ten-year-old.'

'I feel like a ten-year-old.'

'Except,' Heather said slowly, watching her sister with delight, 'that when you were ten you sounded thirty.' She turned to Alastair and her eyes shone with pleasure. 'We can't tell you how much it means to us—that our Penny-Rose met you.'

Alastair smiled, but inside he didn't smile at all. Their pleasure in this marriage made him feel like a traitor. Why? He'd paid for this, he thought grimly. He'd paid money for a bride. So why was he feeling like a rat?

Because they were assuming he was doing this because he loved her, he thought, and he did no such thing. In twelve months he'd walk away.

Back to Belle.

Belle would never come to dinner with sand on her nose, bare toes and a make-up-free face that glowed with happiness, he thought suddenly, watching Rose's lovely, laughing face.

It was just as well. Belle would be a sensible, practical wife.

'Have some lobster,' Penny-Rose said, and handed him a claw. She seemed totally oblivious of his confusion. 'This guy's defending his territory even in death. I can't get the meat out.'

That made him grin. She was in lobster up to her elbows, and her enjoyment was obvious to all. He thought back to the night she'd eaten her first snail, and he knew without asking that this was her first lobster.

'Allow me.' He cracked the shell with practised ease. The long, smooth sliver of meat slid free, and then, because he couldn't resist it, he leaned forward and popped it between her lips. She gazed up at him as the meat disappeared and...

And it was suddenly an incredibly sexy moment, and behind them he heard Heather snigger.

'Um...excuse me, are we in the way?'

'No,' said Penny-Rose, and blushed to the roots of her hair. 'I... Thank you.'

'That's quite all right.' Alastair tried for an unflustered voice but it didn't quite come off. 'Cracking lobsters is one of my splinter skills. Along with swimming lessons.'

And he badly wanted to do it again. Pop a little more lobster between those lips... In fact, he wanted to desperately. But Rose was pushing her plate away decisively.

'Swimming's worse than stone-walling,' she said, and her voice sounded even more flustered than he was feeling. 'I'm going to bed.'

'But there's meringue for dessert.' Mike couldn't believe that she could leave, and

Penny-Rose turned her attention gratefully to her younger brother.

'I'm sure you won't have any trouble eating my share. Or Alastair will help.' And then she caught the way Alastair was looking at her. 'G-goodnight.'

And she fled.

Which left Alastair sitting with her sisters and brother. Who were all looking at him with an air of bright expectancy.

And he couldn't disappoint them. Could he?

'I guess I'll turn in, too,' he said, and they beamed their approval. After all, this was how honeymoons were supposed to proceed.

Help!

But he left anyway. How could he not?

Because Rose was waiting.

This bedroom arrangement was impossible.

When he got back to their cottage, Rose was already in the bathroom. She was running a bath, so there was nothing for Alastair to do but to lie on the bed and listen to her wallowing in the vast white tub.

He could imagine her so vividly she might as well have left the door open. He knew how it would be…

The bathroom was a tiny walled patio with three sheltered walls and the fourth side open to the sea. The bathtub was sunk into the decking. It had two soft headrests, and it was designed so lovers could lie side by side. They could soak in the warm water and watch the moon over the sea.

Only…one side would be empty, Alastair thought. *His* side. The other side would have Rose.

Rose…

He let his imagination wander. Lovely, naked Rose, slippery with soap suds, lying back, letting the salt and sand wash away from her gorgeous body. Penny-Rose lying alone in a bath built for two…

Rose! Not Penny-Rose.

Stop thinking like this! You'll go stark, staring crazy—if you're not already, he said desperately to himself, and took himself out for a walk.

Where could he go? If he walked around the cottage and down to their secluded cove, he'd be able to look up and see…

No. Damn, he was turning into a peeping Tom!

He strode deliberately back up to the management lodge where the kids were setting up a game of cards. From the darkness he could see them out on the verandah, laughing as they played some silly game of snap.

He couldn't go there. What would he say?

'Can I play, too? Your sister's taking a bath and it's driving me nuts!'

They'd think he *was* nuts. They were such nice kids. And they thought he was in love with their sister.

Which was nonsense. He wasn't in love with anyone.

But he was definitely in lust with her.

That was it. He'd found the answer. Only lust. He just wanted her body. He was as aroused as he'd ever been in his life, and the fact that she was a virgin bride...

She was *his* virgin bride.

She wasn't *his* anything. And she had to stay a virgin, he told himself desperately. Hell, wasn't that why he'd married her? Because he didn't want commitment? So it had to stay that way. The last thing he wanted was to make it hard for her to walk away.

But was he sure about what he wanted?

He knew what he didn't want. He didn't want commitment.

In fact, he didn't want marriage. He'd agreed to marry Belle because his mother had wanted grandchildren, he'd quite liked the idea of kids, he'd needed a hostess and the whole thing had been sensible. That was a decent basis for a marriage. Sense.

Not lust.

So he should walk right back to his cottage, settle down on the far side of the pile of cushions and go straight to sleep.

But…he just might take a cold shower first.

A cold shower didn't help.

Alastair returned to the cottage to find Rose glowing from the warmth of the bath. She was wearing one of those damned lingerie-type nightdresses she'd bought in Paris and she was curled into her half of the bed with the sheet drawn up to her waist.

The sheet wasn't drawn up far enough. The nightgown was cut low over her lovely curving breasts, her curls were sprayed out over the pillow—and it was as much as he could do not to groan.

So he stood under the cold shower for a very long time. When he emerged she was lying in the half-dark. Only his bedside light was on. She was still awake, smiling up at him in the dim light as he walked around to his side of the bed.

And heaven only knew how heavy his feet felt. It was so darned hard to make himself walk around her.

This was crazy!

'Feeling better?' she whispered, and he managed a nod.

'Yes. Thanks.' But he'd lied.

'It's been the most gorgeous day,' she said sleepily as he slid down under the sheet—still on his side. 'Thank you, Alastair.'

'Think nothing of it.' That sounded curt. He forced himself to smile, and then flicked off the light so he wouldn't need to hide his expression. But he could still see the curves of her in the moonlight. She was too damned close! 'I enjoyed myself, too.'

'You'd never seen yourself as a swimming master extraordinaire?'

'There's a whole lot of things I'd never seen myself as,' he said bitterly. 'A prince. A swimming master—'

'A husband?'

'The kids think it's real,' he burst out, and there was surely the nub of the matter. If no one thought it was real, he wouldn't have to pretend. It was the pretence that was driving him crazy—wasn't it?

'They do,' she said softly. 'Do you mind?'

'I... No. Only if you do,' he managed. 'It'll make it harder at the end of the year.'

'Alastair, let's worry about the end of the year at the end of the year. For now...this is the honeymoon of my dreams. The holiday of my dreams. I've learned to swim five strokes. I'm here with my sisters and brother—and with you. I couldn't be any happier if I tried.'

He could be. He could be a whole lot happier. All he had to do was shift these damned cushions!

He had to stay formal. Somehow. 'I'm glad you're having a good time.'

'I'm having a wonderful time.' And then, before he knew what she was about, she slipped her hand under the pillows and found his hand. Her fingers were warm and sure as she pulled his hand toward her, and then she raised his hand to her lips and gently kissed his fingertips.

It was a gesture of thanks. Nothing more. Wasn't it?

'This is magic,' she said softly. 'A magic day. A magic prince.'

'It'll end.' He somehow managed to haul his hand away, and it nearly tore him apart to do it. His voice came out as a sort of strangled croak. 'After all, Cinderella had her midnight to contend with. Your midnight is just taking a while longer to come.'

'I won't forget.' Her voice was suddenly serious, but she was still whispering into the dark. The sensation was unutterably intimate. 'Alastair, why are you so afraid of commitment?'

'I'm not.'

'You are.' He heard her smile in her voice. 'You're just a great big chicken.'

He drew in his breath. How to answer that one?

With the truth. 'I'd rather be a chicken than a squashed hen.'

'There's a brave prince.' She chuckled. 'Is that your royal creed? "He who fights and runs away lives to fight another day."'

'It has a whole lot going for it.' It was surreal. Lying in the dark, talking to her as if nothing was between them.

Only these damned cushions!

'Seriously, though…'

'Seriously what?'

'Why don't you let yourself love…Belle?'

Because I've never been the least bit tempted to love Belle, he thought, but he didn't say it. Whereas you…

But he had to give her a reasonable answer. An answer he thought was the truth. 'I've told you before. I don't do love.'

'Because you might get hurt?' Her voice was carefully neutral.

'Because I *will* get hurt. Eventually. Or you...or Belle would. Nothing lasts for ever.'

'So...' She'd forgotten to whisper. Her voice was curious now. Nothing more. 'So when you're designing buildings, you're planning on them lasting a thousand years?' she asked.

'Like your fences?' He smiled into the dark. 'Nope. You're the master builder in that direction.'

'So how long would a building of yours last—on average, say?'

He didn't understand what she was getting at. 'I'd like to think a hundred years.' He shrugged. 'But probably only forty. Maybe less.'

'But you still think it's worthwhile building them.'

Damn. He'd walked straight into her trap. And the cushions weren't high enough!

'Buildings are different,' he managed.

'I imagine they are,' she said softly. 'Different to relationships. But in some ways they're the same. If they only last for forty years they can still be incredibly wonderful while they last.' She frowned then, and he heard the frown in the dark. He was starting to know her so well…

'You lost Lissa,' she said gently. 'You said she was your best friend. Today you told me about teaching her to swim when you were kids. If you had your time again, would you choose not to have that time with her? Because she might die?'

'That's none of your business.' She was cutting too close to the bone here.

'I'm just interested.'

'Well, stop being interested. Go to sleep.'

Ha! That was a good one. How could they possibly sleep?

'I don't think you're being fair on Belle— that's all.' She was still probing, right where it hurt most. 'I think marriage is all about loving someone to bits.'

'Like your father's and mother's marriage?'

'That's not fair.'

'Isn't it?'

'At least they took a chance,' she said, and now she sounded angry. 'At least they tried. They didn't lock themselves up in some antiseptic world in case the big bad love-bug bit them so hard it hurt. So, yes, they loved and,

yes, it did hurt. My mother made a bad marriage but she had four kids and she had a life.
And she loved my dad to bits, even if he was
a loser. She loved him and even when she knew
she was dying, I suspect she never regretted a
thing.'

'Apart from leaving you all.'

'We had her,' Penny-Rose said strongly. 'We
had her for enough time to love her and be
proud to be her kids. Even Michael has the sto-
ries we tell about her, and the knowledge that
he was loved. You think we'd abandon that
love or not embrace it in the first place because
we knew she'd die? If you do, then you don't
know what way your head is screwed on,
Alastair de Castaliae.'

'Oh, for heaven's sake…'

'There's no ''for heaven's sake'' about it.
You loved Lissa. You should try loving Belle.'

'I can't love Belle.'

There. He'd said it. It hung between them,
almost as big a barrier as the cushions.

'Then don't marry her.'

'I'm married to you.'

'No, you're not,' she said reasonably. 'You
can't be married to someone when there's two
feet of cushions between them. That someone

refuses to be married on that basis. This is pretend, Alastair.'

'I... Yes.'

'But you and Belle aren't pretending.'

'We don't need to,' he said, exasperated. 'It's a business arrangement.'

'But...' She reflected on this for a moment. 'You're not paying her.'

'No.'

'And you're intending to have kids?'

'Maybe. Yes! I'll need an heir.'

'Poor little heir,' she said softly. 'I hope Marguerite loves it enough for all of you.'

'I'll love it.'

'No.' Penny-Rose shook her head, and anger vibrated harshly in her voice. 'How can you? Because that's commitment, too. That's risking your precious independence, and you don't want that.'

'Rose...'

'It's Penny-Rose. And what?' she said crossly.

'Can we go to sleep?'

'How can I go to sleep?' she demanded. 'How can I sleep when I've had such a wonderful, wonderful day, and I've learned to swim and I've seen dolphins and I'm now lying in bed wide awake beside the most gorgeous man

I've ever met and…and you expect me to sleep?'

Silence.

Hell, she was feeling the same as he was!

'I…'

'You took a cold shower,' she said carefully. 'I know. The bathroom didn't steam. You think my bath was hot?'

'Rose—'

'This is impossible,' she snapped. 'Cold showers aren't all they're cracked up to be. I'm going nuts, and there's twelve months to go. You'd better take me home to your castle and dig a few moats. Right through the middle of the castle. And fill the moats with alligators—with you on one side and me on the other. Because this year's getting out of hand already.'

Alastair tried reason. 'Rose, if we're sensible—'

And that was enough for her. She sat up, and in the dim light he could see her eyes flashing with temper. 'Why the hell do we need to be sensible?'

'Because…'

'Because why?' A cushion tumbled toward her and she lifted it and hurled it to the other side of the room. 'Stupid cushion.'

'Rose—'

'Don't "Rose" me.' She was so angry she was almost spitting. 'OK. Here's the truth. I didn't want to do this—I didn't want to tell you—but it's too much for me to hide and I can't go around like you—an ostrich with my head in the sand—for twelve months.'

'I don't know what you mean.'

But he did.

'You can't feel this thing between us?'

'No!'

'Liar.'

The word hung in the air between them. A threat...

The truth.

And then she'd had enough. She took a deep breath and she said what she'd promised not to say. Whatever the outcome, it had to be said.

'I love you, Alastair de Castaliae,' she said, and her anger was all around them. She was furious with him. She was also furious with herself for betraying what she hadn't wanted to reveal. But there was suddenly no choice.

He was so close.

And there were these stupid cushions!

Another cushion went flying.

'I love you,' she repeated. 'I know. It's stupid. Stupid, stupid, stupid. But you picked me up and rescued me from a life of poverty, you took me to Paris and fed me snails and cheeses and strawberries, you bought me the sexiest knickers a girl could ever have—and then refused to look at them. And you rescued me from traffic and you gave me the most gorgeous dog...'

That was a good one. The most gorgeous dog...

'Are we talking about Leo here?' he asked cautiously, and she glared and threw away another cushion. She was tempted to whop him with it.

'Shut up.' She glowered. 'Just listen. And then you take my little brother as your best man and you stand there in your gorgeous suit and you smile at me, and you make *those* vows! *And you give me copestones for a wedding present.* Damn, a girl would have to be abnormal to ignore that, and I'm not abnormal. I'm truly, madly, deeply in love with you. So there. I've said it. You can do with it what you like, Your Serene Stupid Highness. Like it or lump it.'

Her breath caught on a sob. 'And you needn't worry that it changes anything. At the end of the year I'll still walk away as I promised. But for what it's worth, you should know what you're letting go. You have a wife. I might not be the wife you planned, but I'm a wife all the same. Not a pretend wife, Alastair. I'm a wife who loves you so much it hurts, and who's given you her heart and who doesn't expect a single thing in return.'

And she flung herself over onto her breast and buried her face in her remaining pillows.

And then she sat up again and swallowed. The situation was impossible and somehow she had to strive for lightness.

'Except another swimming lesson tomorrow,' she managed, while Alastair stared at her in open-mouthed amazement. 'I do expect that. You know, this doesn't mean anything has to change, but I thought you ought to know the facts—and the facts are that I'm yours. If you want me. But if you don't want me then that's OK, too. As long as I get to swim tomorrow.'

And that was the end of that.

She buried her head again, and Alastair sat staring down at her, trying to figure out what the hell to say.

What was there to say?

He could think of exactly nothing.

CHAPTER ELEVEN

ALASTAIR slept on the beach.

Or rather he tossed and turned on the beach. He'd taken a spare blanket and gone down to the sand. Back in the cottage, his wife's body had been rigid. Her breathing had been even and measured but he'd known she hadn't been asleep and there would have been no sleep for either of them if he'd stayed where he was.

So he'd left, and lay in the moonlight and listened to the waves gently lap the shore—and wondered what on earth he had done and where he could go from here.

Back to Rose, his body screamed at him. He had only to make the slightest move...

She...*loved him*?

Nonsense. That was impossible. Fantasy stuff. He'd let himself get too close, he told himself, and she was too alone in the world. She'd built him into something he couldn't be.

He'd never pretended with her. She knew him...

She knew what she wanted to know. Love? It'd fade. Romantic love. Ha!

But…his mother and father had been in love, and their love had endured for over thirty years.

And then it had been shattered in one instant, he remembered bitterly. One drunken driver on a motorway and that love had been splintered into a thousand shards, each one capable of hurting to death…

His mother had shrivelled since his father's death. And so had he.

Lissa had accepted a ride from Paris with Alastair's father, and the two had been wiped out in milliseconds. Love lost…

Love found? Rose was back in their cottage, waiting. Waiting for her husband.

All he had to do was take her, he thought savagely. It would be so easy. To accept her love.

But he was incapable of giving that love in return. Because he knew that giving meant pain. He couldn't… He just couldn't expose himself to that sort of pain again! No matter how desirable she was, he couldn't take that last final step. He couldn't depend on her for his sanity.

And he surely would depend on her if he let himself believe in her loving. It would be so easy to lay his life in her sweet hands.

To love and lose... That was the way of madness!

So he was better here, under the stars. For twelve months, if necessary. For however long it took for this strange marriage to run its course.

Penny-Rose came to find him just before dawn.

He was half awake, half asleep, and his dark form was a mere shadow on the sand. She came flying down to the beach and almost fell over him. As he reached up and steadied her, she fell to her knees.

'Alastair...'

And all of a sudden things had changed. There was no hint of the passion—or the anger—of the night before. There was only fear in her voice, and the fear was raw and real.

'What is it?' He was sitting up, and she was kneeling, still in the lovely negligee of last night, her curls tumbled and wild and her eyes huge in the pre-dawn light.

'Alastair...'

'Just say it.'

'Alastair, it's your mother.'

Marguerite had had a heart attack. The call had come through to the resort, and the manager had come to the cottage to break the news.

'My...my husband's gone for a dawn walk,' Penny-Rose had managed. 'Just tell me what's wrong, and I'll find him.'

So now she told Alastair what the manager had told her.

'Marguerite went back to Paris the day after we were married,' she explained gently. 'But apparently she's had chest pains, and they've been growing worse. Finally she made an appointment to see her local doctor, but by the time she reached him it was a full-stage heart attack. She's in Intensive Care.'

'I'll go.' Alastair was rising, and Penny-Rose was right there with him.

'I'll come with you.'

But Alastair was no longer seeing her. His thoughts were only on his mother. 'I'll find the manager and see how fast I can get back to Paris.'

Getting back to Paris was easier said than done. The supply boat pulled into the island once a week, bringing the guests from the mainland. Otherwise they came by helicopter.

'And the hire chopper's out of action,' the manager said apologetically. By the time Penny-Rose and Alastair reached his office, he'd already made enquiries on their behalf.

'The engine's being reconditioned. I'm afraid it's useless until Thursday.'

'That's two days.' Alastair took a deep breath. 'You mean there's no way I can get off the island until then? I can pay the boat.'

'The boat does the rounds of the islands. It'll take at least a day to get back here. But if I could make a suggestion…'

'Anything.'

'One of the outer islands is owned by a re-clusive fisherman.' The manager gave a dep-recating smile. 'A rich, reclusive fisherman. He's somewhat of an eccentric. He lives alone and doesn't socialise. But he owns his own helicopter.'

Alastair frowned. 'Will he rent it out?'

'Maybe, but it only holds one passenger.' The manager cast an apologetic glance at Penny-Rose. 'And while I might be able to per-suade him to make a mercy dash for one, I doubt he'd take kindly to doing more.'

'That's fine. It's only me that's going.'

'But…' Penny-Rose flinched. 'Alastair, I need to go with you.'

'There's no room,' he said briefly. 'And no need either.'

He didn't need her. Of course he didn't. Penny-Rose's face tightened. But it was Marguerite she was worried about. Wasn't it?

Damn it, she was worried about both of them. And if anything happened to Marguerite and she wasn't by Alastair's side...

'I'd still like to come.'

'I'm afraid you can't, ma'am,' the resort manager apologised. 'At least, not straight away.' He lifted the telephone and looked enquiringly at Alastair. 'The plane from Suva to Europe leaves at nine this morning. That means there's very little time. If I make fast arrangements I can have you on it.'

'Do it,' Alastair growled. He turned and found Rose watching him. She looked...

Hell, she looked like she'd been kicked. And like she was expecting to be kicked again.

'The kids are booked back to Australia on Saturday,' he told her, his voice gentling. 'That's when the boat calls. You can't cut it short. You know this is the holiday they've always dreamed of, and so have you.'

He couldn't resist then. He put a hand out to trace the outline of her cheek, and if it had been meant to comfort her, then who could blame him if he took a modicum of comfort himself?

'Have a wonderful time. Come back when they leave.'

'You don't want me.'

'I don't...need you.'

And that was that.

'Belle?'

'Alastair...' It was early evening in Paris.

Alastair telephoned Belle's cellphone while he sat in the departure lounge at Suva, and she answered on the first ring. There was a party of some sort in the background. He could hear laughter and voices and the clink of glasses...

'Alastair, what is it?'

Briefly he outlined what had happened, and she was horrified.

'Oh, Alastair, that's dreadful. You poor darling...'

He didn't want sympathy for himself. That was the last thing he needed. He wanted tangible help.

'Belle, she's alone. You know we have no family in Paris, and my only aunt's in Yorkshire and too frail to travel. It'll take me twenty-four hours to get there. Please... can you go to her?'

'Visit her in hospital, you mean.'

'Yes,' he said gratefully. 'Belle, I know it's a lot to ask, but could you stay with her until I get there? I can't bear to think of her being alone. Of her being in pain...'

'Of course I'll go, darling.' He heard her pause and speak an aside to someone in the background, and then she came on the line again. 'Sorry about that. Damn clients. Just tell me what hospital she's in and as soon as my guests leave I'll go.'

'Not now?'

'Alastair, these are important clients—'

He said something exceedingly rude about the clients.

She didn't appreciate it. 'Alastair! There's no need to be coarse. I'll go as soon as I can.'

And that was all he could do.

Twenty minutes later, the jet lifted off from the international airport, and Alastair was finally away. The plane circled the islands underneath as it veered to face Europe.

And Alastair stared down at the turquoise sea and imagined his wife. Rose. She'd be practising her swimming, he thought, and wondered if she'd have made it past five strokes by the next time he saw her.

She would—and he'd miss seeing her try.

The thought was suddenly almost unbearable. He stared down into the water, willing himself to see, but it was too far away.

But he stayed looking for a very long time.

But Penny-Rose wasn't swimming. As Alastair's helicopter took off for the mainland she sat and watched until the sound had faded to nothing, the seabirds had returned to reclaim the patch of beach where the helicopter had landed and the machine was far out of sight.

Yet still she watched.

Have a wonderful time, he'd said.

How could she do that when Marguerite might be dying? When anything could be happening on the other side of the world.

On *her* side of the world.

And that was the crux of it. This wasn't her home. And neither was Australia. Home was where the heart was.

Home was with Alastair.

Fiji. Los Angeles. London. Paris.

The journey was interminable. Each step seemed to take for ever and sleep was impossible. By the time Alastair reached the hospital he was past the point of rational thinking. So much time had elapsed. What if...?

'What if' didn't bear thinking of. At least Belle was with her, he thought again and again. If the worst came to the worst, his mother wouldn't be completely alone.

But, thankfully, the worst hadn't come to the worst.

'She's had a mild heart attack.' The physician on duty saw the grey look of strain in his face, and answered his overriding terror straight away. 'She's still very much alive and she should be OK—'

'Should?' He went straight to the nub of the matter. 'Why do you say *should*?'

The physician gave him a smile that didn't quite reassure him. 'The attack itself didn't cause long-term damage, but we've had to operate. One of her arteries has become too thin to allow safe passage of blood. The way it was, it was a miracle she hadn't had an attack earlier. I'm sure she's been suffering angina for some time. She wanted to wait until you arrived but we daren't. In fact, she's in Theatre right now.'

The physician's voice gentled as she tried to ease his strain. 'She's having what's called a coronary artery bypass, and there's every reason to hope she'll come through it with flying colours.'

'But...' Alastair's eyes were searching the doctor's face. 'She mightn't?'

'Your mother is seventy. She's been ill, and it's a major operation. There's always a chance that things won't go well.'

'She could die on the operating table?'

'Yes,' the doctor said frankly. 'There is that chance. But there's every reason to hope that she won't.'

'I wish I could have been here—before she went in.'

'We couldn't wait,' the physician told him. 'I'm sorry.'

Alastair put his hands up and raked his hair, then closed his eyes. 'At least she had Belle.' He opened his eyes again, forcing himself to practicalities. If his mother was in Theatre, there was nothing to do but find Belle. 'Where's she waiting?'

'Belle?'

'My...our friend.' As the doctor looked confused, Alastair explained further. 'Belle will be here somewhere. I rang her...' he glanced at his watch '...twenty-four hours ago.'

'As far as I know, there's been no one with your mother.'

Silence.

'You're kidding.'

'I've spent a lot of time with your mother,' the physician told him. 'I've been on duty in Coronary Care for the last twelve hours.' She gave a rueful smile. 'We've had an epidemic of heart attacks and I've hardly had a break. I would have seen anyone with your mother.'

He couldn't believe it. 'Belle said she'd come.'

'Maybe she's been delayed,' the doctor said gently. She, too, glanced at her watch. Her time with Alastair was over. 'It may well be a couple of hours before your mother's out of Theatre. Can I show you where you can wait, or would you prefer to find yourself a hotel, freshen up and come back when the surgery's finished?'

'I'll wait,' Alastair said grimly. 'Of course I'll wait.'

He waited for four hours. The surgery went on for ever, and Alastair paced the waiting room as if somehow expending energy could help. It didn't.

'There are complications.' The physician popped in to find him before she finally went off duty. 'I'm sorry, but it's taking longer than expected.'

'But—'

'There's still no need to panic,' she reassured him. 'Not yet. It's just been a more extensive repair job than they thought.'

'She'll never make it,' Alastair groaned, and the doctor looked at him and then pushed him gently into a chair.

'Sit,' she ordered. 'I'll ask the staff to bring you sandwiches and coffee.' And then she paused. 'Is there anyone you want us to contact? You mentioned a name before. Belle? Would you like her to be with you?'

'No!'

And suddenly he was very sure of it.

And he was also sure who he really wanted to be by his side.

He wanted his Penny-Rose.

And he wanted her so badly it was as if his heart were as injured as his mother's.

Belle arrived half an hour later, breezing into the waiting room with her arms full of flowers as if she were there to visit a mother with a newborn babe. She looked gorgeous. Chic and immaculate in a tiny black suit that must have cost a mint, not a hair out of place, her face immaculately made up...

Here was every reason he had wanted to marry her, Alastair thought grimly. She was indeed the perfect woman.

So why, as she gave a cry of pleasure, placed her flowers aside and rushed to put her arms around him, did he feel nothing? Nothing at all.

It was as if she were some sort of plastic doll—beautiful, but inside there was nothing.

She didn't notice his reaction. 'Oh, Alastair, what a frightful time you must have had. Poor darling.' She kissed him lightly, then pulled away and made a little moue with her lips. 'Darling, you haven't shaved.'

He hadn't. And he didn't give a damn.

'Has it taken twenty-four hours,' he said carefully, 'for you to decide what to wear when visiting hospital?'

She looked astounded. 'I'm sorry?'

'Where the hell have you been?' His pent-up anxiety exploded in fury. 'I asked you to come. I needed someone to be here with her. What have you been doing?'

'Darling, I knew you couldn't be here until now.'

'I asked you to see my mother. Not me.'

She still looked astonished, as if the idea of spending time with an old lady was preposterous. 'I rang.'

'You rang?'

'Of course I rang.' Belle was defensive and angry in return. She had never been one to take criticism lightly. 'The nurse said she was as well as could be expected and due for surgery. There wasn't any point in coming while she was busy having pre-op examinations and things. I would have just had to sit in the room and wait.'

'Right.' He was past anger now. He was cold and drained and very, very tired. 'What a waste of time. Of course. So when she went to Theatre, she had no one with her at all.'

'She had the staff.'

'It's not the same, Belle.' He drew in an angry breath and he knew what he had to say. 'She had no one with her who loved her. It's important.'

'I don't...'

'You don't love my mother? Of course you don't.' He nodded, his weariness intensifying by the minute. 'I should have thought of that.'

'I'm fond of Marguerite,' she chided him gently. 'Alastair, you're weary. You're not thinking straight.'

'Maybe I am.' He shook his head, trying to clear the fog, but truth was surrounding him, fog or not. He lifted the flowers from the table and handed them back to her. 'Love is... important. I hadn't realised it. Until now. And we don't have it, Belle.'

'What—?'

'We never have had it,' he said grimly. 'And I want it. I want it for my mother, for my children—and for me. And I won't find it with you. So...' He took a deep breath. 'I'm sorry, Belle, but there it is. I organised my life like a business. But it's not like that. Since Lissa died—'

'Alastair, I understand—'

'You don't,' he said bleakly. 'After Lissa died I thought I could do without love. But that was because I didn't know what love was. Not true love. Lissa and I were the best of friends and her death hurt like hell. Maybe if we'd married we would have ended up loving...like it's possible to love. Maybe we wouldn't. All I know is that when I made my vow not to love, I didn't have a clue what I was talking about. I do now.'

She still didn't get it. 'Darling, you're overwrought.'

'I'm overwrought,' he agreed. 'Yes. And maybe I should have been overwrought a long time ago. Take your flowers, Belle,' he told her. 'I'm sorry if I've messed with the smooth running of your life, but there's no future for us. Take your flowers and go.'

She got it then. Her eyes narrowed in anger. 'Oh, Alastair, for heaven's sake. If that little slut has pulled you in—'

'If you're talking about my wife, I'd advise you to be very, very careful,' he growled. 'My wife is anything but a slut.' He took a deep breath. 'My wife is my love.'

Marguerite came back from Theatre two hours later and they still didn't know if she'd make it. She had tubes and machines hooked up everywhere and the sight of her pale face made Alastair feel sick.

'She arrested on the operating table,' the surgeon explained. 'We've been very lucky to get her back. But the repair work has been done. If she pulls through the next few hours she should be fine.'

So he sat, glued to her bedside, willing her to keep on breathing.

Hour after hour.

Staff came and went. He hardly noticed. All he saw was his mother. All he thought about was his mother.

Or maybe that wasn't quite true. Because at the back of his mind was an aching need for Penny-Rose.

Why was he calling her Penny-Rose in his thoughts?

It was how he'd first seen her, he thought. Diminutive and work-stained and determined. Clad in overalls, ready to take on the world for her siblings, as tough as old boots.

And tender to the core.

She'd said she loved him.

Hell!

He watched his mother, but over and over through that dreadful night he thought of his wife.

And with the dawn, Marguerite opened her eyes and smiled.

'Alastair.' It was a faint whisper, thready and weak, but she was there, conscious and alive. Her pleasure resonated in her voice. 'What…what are you doing here?'

'I came to be with you.'

'But…' She thought that through. 'You should be with your wife.'

'Penny-Rose…' It was so close to what he'd been thinking that he was thrown off balance.

'You know it's just make-believe. Penny-Rose isn't my wife.'

'Of course she is.' Marguerite squeezed his hand with what little strength she had. 'She loves you just like I loved your father. She loves you even more than I love you. So much...'

And she closed her eyes and slept—and left him wondering.

Finally he was persuaded to take a break. Marguerite was settled, her breathing was deep and even and the doctor said she might well sleep for hours. He was sure now that when she woke she'd remember he'd been here, and the staff were smiling their reassurance and their pleasure. She'd live.

So...a shave and a wash and a sleep were called for. Not necessarily in that order.

'But maybe you'd better see your friend before you go,' the charge nurse said, and he frowned.

'My friend?'

'She's in the main waiting room. She says you won't want to see her—that we're not to disturb you—but she's been waiting for some time now. Maybe seven or eight hours. She looks as worried as you have been. I was just about to send someone down to tell her your mother has every chance of recovering, but if you'd like to tell her yourself...'

It didn't make sense. 'Belle's been waiting?'

'Is that her name? She didn't say. You'll find her down the hall.'

So he went down the hall—and in the waiting room was Penny-Rose.

For a moment he said nothing—just stood staring down at her as if he were seeing an apparition. The waiting room was deserted—no one but the most anxious of relatives would be here at this early hour. So Penny-Rose had sat alone and her eyes had been glued to the door as she'd waited.

When Alastair appeared, she looked up at him without saying a word. Her eyes were huge, questioning and terrified, and he realised with a stabbing certainty that she wasn't concerned about him. Not now.

Unlike Belle, who'd only come to the hospital when she'd been sure of seeing Alastair, all Penny-Rose's thoughts were with Marguerite. That was what she was searching for in his face. Marguerite's fate. And he looked haggard, he knew, and his face must give the worst of impressions.

But for the life of him he couldn't make himself smile.

All he could think of was that she was there. She was his love. The two thoughts crashed down on him with overwhelming force.

How could he have been so stupid as not to have seen it? How could he have thought he couldn't love?

Here she was. Miraculously here. His wonderful, wonderful bride. His wife!

'Penny-Rose...' His voice came out a haggard whisper, and she came straight to the worst conclusion possible.

'Oh, Alastair. Alastair...' It was a whisper of distress and absolute, desolate loss, and she buried her head in her hands and closed her eyes. 'Oh, no.'

He couldn't bear it. It took half a second to cross the room, kneel before her and take those beloved hands in his. To drag her fingers away from her tear-drenched eyes and make her look at him.

'No. Penny-Rose, no! She's alive. She's OK...' As she still looked at him with the remains of horror, he finally made himself smile. 'Sweetheart, I didn't mean to look dreadful. It's just because I haven't shaved and haven't slept. But she's recovering. They've operated and they've repaired the damage. She's woken, she's spoken to me and I've left her to sleep.'

She stared up at him, torn between disbelief and hope. Her eyes were vast pools of exhausted misery. Weariness had put her almost past hope.

But, finally, hope won.

'You mean...she'll live?'

'Yes.'

'You're sure?'

'As sure as I can be. I wouldn't have left her otherwise.'

'Oh, Alastair.'

It was too much. She put her arms around his neck, buried her face in his shoulder and burst into tears.

He didn't let her stay there. Not for long anyway.

For maybe a minute he let her weep, while wonder faded and her touch seeped into his soul. She was real. She was here.

She was his.

And he could wait no longer. He put her back from him, looked at her drowning face and smiled down into her eyes with a smile that held infinite tenderness, infinite wonder—and infinite love.

'My Penny-Rose,' he said softly. 'My love.'

And his mouth found hers, and he kissed her with a passion that threatened to last for ever.

It was a kiss that made a marriage—a marriage that was from this moment forward.

'How did you get here?'

Neither of them knew how long it took before words were possible between them, but when they were, everything that needed to be said somehow already had been. The kiss had said it all. Penny-Rose was in her husband's arms and it would take the strength of giants to tear her away. 'How on earth did you do it?'

'Magic.' She smiled, and he chuckled.

'I know. More of the fairy godmother stuff. But seriously...'

'Seriously, the resort manager realised how much I wanted to go so he contacted your recluse with the helicopter and used all his charm to persuade him to take me as well. Of course, we didn't make it to Suva in time for your flight, so I caught a flight back to Sydney, then flew to Singapore and on to Paris. I must have landed only about five or six hours after you.'

He stared at her in astonishment. 'You must be exhausted.'

'No more than you.' She was snuggled into him, settled and happy. Happy wasn't a big enough word. Ecstatic!

'But why did you come? You wanted the holiday so much.'

'Do you think I wanted a holiday more than being here...with you?' She was indignant. 'And with Marguerite. If anything had happened to Marguerite and I hadn't been here...'

'For me?'

Penny-Rose looked up at him, her face deadly serious. 'For you,' she agreed. But... Alastair, I love your mother.'

'It's your speciality,' he said softly. 'Giving and giving and giving.'

That puzzled her. 'I don't have anything to give.'

'And I do?' His voice was incredulous—angry even. 'Money, riches, power—sure, I have all of those things. I have so much to give. Just not the thing that counts. Love.'

'But you can't—'

'I couldn't.' He kissed her again, because he couldn't bear not to. Heavens, she still tasted like the sea. It'd be the salt of her tears, he knew, but the smell of her, the feel of her...

She was like the sea and the sky and the heavens all rolled into one.

How had he ever thought he could put her away from him after a year? How had he ever thought he could keep himself from her for a year?

'I can love now,' he said, and all the joy of the morning was in his voice. 'I've learned. I've had the very best of teachers. Oh, Rose…my Penny-Rose…'

Her face clouded, just a little, at the memories the name brought back. 'Penny-Rose?'

'I've been really stupid,' he told her. 'Trying to make you into something that you weren't. But Penny-Rose is how I first saw you. Dressed in those damned overalls, filthy, yet laughing at us, letting us know your values weren't ours. Telling me that a marriage without love was stupid.' He pulled her tightly against him. 'So Rose is a princess. My Princess Rose. But Penny-Rose is the woman I love more than life itself.'

She looked up into his eyes for a long, long moment. And then she sighed with pure happiness.

'Penny-Rose it is,' she said softly. 'I'll go for Penny-Rose any day.'

'You mean you'd rather be the woman I love than a princess?'

'I'd rather be the woman you love than anything in the world.'

'Then so be it,' he said exultantly. 'From this day forth. Because that's exactly what you are.'

And he gathered her against him and kissed her—for a very, very long time.

EPILOGUE

MY WEDDING day. My proper wedding day. A ceremony just for us—with the priest and Alastair and me and Leo. Because we want it to be a proper wedding, there'll be Marguerite and our cameraman to act as witnesses, but there'll be no one else.

A true and legal wedding... It's funny how I'm more nervous now than I was at the big one.

There'll be no velvet coats for Leo today. Or any fancy wedding gowns. We're wearing jeans and bare toes on a beach in the South of France. Where no one knows us. Where we can take each other as we mean to have each other—in the privacy of ourselves.

Just us.

For now and for ever.

'Wilt thou have this woman to be thy wedded wife, to live for ever according to God's law in the Holy estate of matrimony? Wilt thou love her, comfort her, honour and keep her in sickness and in health; and forsaking all others,

286

keep thee only unto her, so long as ye both shall live?'

'I do,' said Alastair.

'And you, Penny-Rose. Wilt thou have this man...?'

'I do,' said Penny-Rose.

'Amen to that,' said Marguerite. Completely recovered, she stood with pride as their witness and she couldn't stop smiling.

'Woof,' said Leo.

'Bless you both,' said their lone cameraman—the man they'd asked to record this event for their great-grandchildren. 'May you be as happy and successful as you've made me.'

And that was the way it was.

MILLS & BOON® PUBLISH EIGHT LARGE PRINT TITLES A MONTH. THESE ARE THE EIGHT TITLES FOR JANUARY 2003

A PASSIONATE SURRENDER
Helen Bianchin

THE HEIRESS BRIDE
Lynne Graham

HIS VIRGIN MISTRESS
Anne Mather

TO MARRY McALLISTER
Carole Mortimer

MISTAKEN MISTRESS
Margaret Way

THE BEDROOM ASSIGNMENT
Sophie Weston

THE PREGNANCY BOND
Lucy Gordon

A ROYAL PROPOSITION
Marion Lennox